The Wrong Seat

an anthology
by the Brookfield and La Grange Writers Groups

Edited by Marie Anderson

Contributing Editors
Kevin M. Folliard

Sally Anderson
Bonny Kotapish
Lauryn Kotapish
Laurie Whitman

Cover by: Margo Rife and Jessica Myers

To the public libraries in Brookfield, IL and La Grange, IL with gratitude from the La Grange and Brookfield Writers Groups: Thank you for giving local writers a welcoming and supportive place to meet and workshop.

Contents

Introduction

I work as a lunchtime supervisor at a grade school. There is a table along a wall in the lunchroom where the supervisors put their coats.

After one shift, I grabbed my puffy black jacket and put it on while chatting with another lunch lady. As always, I reached into the jacket pockets for my gloves and keys.

They weren't there.

My fingers closed around something I'd never owned, never used.

My colleague stopped talking mid-sentence. She frowned. "Marie," she said. "What's happened to your coat?"

I shook my head, feeling like I'd been transported to *The Twilight Zone*. My coat not only had the wrong pockets, it had grown by nearly a foot.

"This isn't my coat!" I exclaimed.

But there were no coats left on the table. Where was *my* coat?

"Mrs. B was wearing a puffy black coat on the playground," my lunch buddy said. "Maybe she grabbed yours by mistake?"

Mrs. B is the gym teacher who occasionally works the lunch shift with us. So we hurried to the gym where we found her organizing fourth graders into volleyball teams.

Sure enough, I had her coat. My coat was in her office, where she'd tossed it before rushing to the gym.

We swapped coats. My keys and gloves were safe and sound in my coat pockets.

A week later, walking out of a writers group meeting, I told my wrong coat story to a few fellow writers. They shared their own wrong coat experiences, and one writer proposed that we all write something on that theme.

This book is the result. All but one of the contributions are fiction. Each piece was workshopped by the writing group, then revised, reviewed, and edited, often several times, until author and editor agreed that the final version was, indeed, the final version.

I loved seeing these stories and poems evolve into their final versions. I love the variety of interpretations of one simple theme.

We—editors and contributors—all hope that you, our readers, will enjoy them too.

Oh, and what did I find in the pockets of Mrs. B's coat?

I won't say.

—Marie Anderson
Anthology Editor

The Wrong Coat

stories and poems
by members of
The Brookfield Library Writers Group
&
The La Grange Library Writers Group

John Quinn
My Jacket, Oh My Jacket

I was badly in need of a haircut, but when I got to the barber shop, it was crowded. That was okay. I had my *Sports Illustrated Magazine (SI)* with me and the whole cold and gusty and rainy afternoon in front of me. The barber shop offered shelter, light, and free coffee, as well as the dusty scent of talcum and pomade.

After registering with an elderly gentleman, I found a hook on the wall for my new White Sox jacket. It nestled proudly with other jackets, raincoats, and sweaters. There was a chair in the corner. I waded through the muddle, sat and settled in for a warm, dry wait.

The shop was populated with males and mothers of males. There must have been twenty people queuing for six barbers, but that was okay. Three young boys, surly and capricious, were obliterating the normal adult drone of the shop while their mothers nodded and smiled.

I should pay attention to omens.

The feature article in *SI* was on the Chicago baseball scene and tried to compare the South Side battlers, my White Sox, to the Cubs, pansies of the North Side. There was, of course, little to compare. However, the author tried to seem even-handed, God bless him, even if he knew little about baseball and Chicago.

I chuckled, smirked, and smiled as I compared the unbalanced records of the two Chicago teams, from the Truman presidency to the present. Finally, my name was called and I found a chair with a barber who was a real baseball fan, I mean a real, real baseball fan, a season ticket holder for Sundays at "The Cell," home of the Sox. His name was Luke, named after Luke Appling, erstwhile star shortstop of the 1940s. He nodded as he clipped and, as an extremely knowledgeable fan, agreed with everything I said. He was munching on every word I uttered as he snipped away.

He earned a sizable tip. I paid, shook my barber's hand, and went to retrieve my jacket.

It was gone.

The crowd had thinned. There were four people in barber chairs, and no one, but a mother calming a tot, waiting. The line of hooks held two rain coats, each large enough to cover an infield during a rain delay. They obviously belonged to two elderly gentlemen who may have played offensive line for the Chicago Bears, or modeled for a dirigible design. There was a child's jacket and a hoody.

And there, on a far hook, a hook closest to the shadows of the corner, dangled a raggedy blue jacket with red and white trim. I felt before I knew, sensed before I saw: the logo was Chicago Cubs. My scream was genuine.

"Oh! My God!" I trembled. "Someone stole my jacket, and look! Look at what they left!" I couldn't touch it. I pointed my quaking finger. The rag hung limply, cowering in the corner. The wind outside was screeching. The temperature of the world was plummeting. The rain had mutated to a mix of slush and sleet.

My barber took my name and number, promised to make it good. He suggested I take the offensive piece of cloth as a temporary solution.

I sneered. "I've walked further in colder weather than this. I'm less than a mile from home. I have my pride." And with that, I stepped outside into the arctic afternoon.

Sally Anderson
To Tell the Truth

"Shelby! You forgot your hat."

A willowy almond skinned girl turned to see her mother waving a pink knit hat out the door. She ran back up the stairs of the brick bungalow to a thin woman whose once golden brown skin had faded to an ashy gray.

"I thought I put it in my pocket."

"If your pocket is the closet floor, then that's exactly where you put it."

Shelby stepped into the door, moving her mother out of the cold air into the warmth of the small entrance. Her mother pulled the hat securely over Shelby's thick naturally wavy locks. *She looks so sick*, Shelby thought.

Her mother tilted her head upward. She placed a kiss just under the bill of Shelby's cap and gave it a tug to secure it on top of her head. "Mama's gonna be fine."

Shelby grabbed her mother tight around her waist. "I love you, Mama."

"I love you, too, baby girl."

Her mother loosened Shelby's grip. "You go on now. Sheila is going to pick you up from school. Then she's gonna take you to get us takeout from your favorite restaurant, The Chinese Kitchen!"

"If Sheila's buying, then I'm getting shrimp with lobster sauce!"

"Don't be so hard on your big sister." Her mother smiled through a cough.

"Well, she likes spending her money."

"Get going so you don't miss your bus." She pulled Shelby's coat close around her neck.

"Ms. Darlene won't leave without me."

"Ms. Darlene has a bus schedule to keep."

"Or, I could stay home?" Shelby produced her best pouty face.

"Not if you want shrimp and lobster sauce for dinner. Sheila's here with me. So you're going to school."

Shelby's eyes rolled back when she heard her sister's name again. She reluctantly stepped onto the porch and descended to the sidewalk. She paused at the end of the walkway. "Sheila better not start another argument with you."

"Go! Now!" her mother prodded from the doorway.

Thoughts churned in Shelby's mind as her pace increased to make up time. She was cutting it close today. If she missed her bus, she'd be late for school. Her new high school was nice, but she'd rather take her classes online so she could take care of her mother. Sheila only thought about herself. Every time she came home, all she did was start arguments with their mother.

A blinking red hand stopped Shelby at the busy intersection a block from her home. *Mama's fine*, Shelby told herself. She felt her face relax into a smile, remembering Mama's favorite story: how Shelby's birth had been such a blessing. *At least Mama has one good daughter,* Shelby decided.

Sheila was fifteen when Shelby was born. When Sheila turned 18, she left for college at NYU and didn't come home often. When she did, she always started fights with their parents. Shelby grew up like an only child—and she liked it that way.

Sheila had made her life and career in New York and occasionally called home and stopped in when business brought her to Chicago. She sent Shelby a constant stream of packages. Once or twice a month, a box would arrive with things her rich big sister thought her poor little sister couldn't live without.

Shelby felt tears puddle her eyes. Two years ago when her mother found out she had cancer, her father was there to keep things going. Sheila came once the whole time, only to leave not speaking to their father.

Her daddy wasn't here anymore. She slapped her tears away in anger. Her father had died in a car accident a month before she graduated eighth grade. Sheila came home never having made up with their father but bearing gifts. Who brings gifts to a funeral? Stuff would never make her take Sheila's side over their parents'.

The light blinked "walk." Shelby ran across the street and boarded the idling city bus parked at its turnaround spot alongside the donut shop.

"Good morning, Ms. Darlene!" Shelby felt her spirits lift.

"Good morning, Shelby. You out here with no gloves?"

"I thought they were in my coat pocket. I hope I didn't lose them."

4

"You teenage girls! I buy my daughter at least two pair of gloves every year." Ms. Darlene closed the bus door behind Shelby and pulled off.

Shelby balanced herself and searched the back of the bus until she spotted a man dressed in a tan cashmere overcoat. A pink and blue tie peeked from the coat's neckline. Her stomach growled relief when she saw Mr. Cliff holding up a bag and cup.

"Hey Shelby-Shoe! It's cold out there. I thought you might like some hot chocolate and a donut."

Mr. Cliff had started calling her Shelby-Shoe a few months ago. Shelby's gym shoe had fallen out of her backpack when she got off the bus one morning. He found it and returned it to her on their ride back home, and their friendship was forged.

"Thanks, Mr. Cliff. This is right on time! Sheila *cooked* breakfast this morning," Shelby said, wiggling her fingers to put air quotes around *cooked*. She dug into the bag and bit the warm old-fashioned buttermilk donut. A sip of the hot chocolate melted the donut in her mouth.

"Don't be so hard on your sister."

"You sound like my mom."

"She's here helping your mom and *you* out."

Shelby turned up her nose. "As soon as my mom gets better, Sheila will be gone back to New York."

"What's with that face! My niece makes that same face. You told me your sister got you that coat. That's a nice coat. Designer." Mr. Cliff touched the posh label imprinted on Shelby's shoulder.

"Yeah, but she has the same one. You know how stupid we look when we go someplace? If my mama wasn't sick, I'd make her take me to get another one."

Shelby hated that coat no matter how much it cost or how "in" it was.

"You're family. She's just trying to bond with you guys."

"I wouldn't care if my mom had the same coat, it's . . ."

"I know. It's Sheila. Maybe she's trying to make up for not being around when you were growing up. With your dad gone and now your mom's sick again." Mr. Cliff gave Shelby a playful nudge with his elbow.

"Well, we're fine without her." Shelby unzipped the puffy jacket and stuck her hand into the inside pocket. "See! This isn't even my coat." She pulled out several pieces of paper. "This is Sheila's stupid coat. She's always writing notes and lists leaving them everywhere."

"Cut her a little slack."

Shelby sifted through the pieces of paper. Words written in block letters caught her eye: TELL SHELBY THE TRUTH. Shelby felt a quizzical look cross her face.

"You okay?" Mr. Cliff asked.

"Yeah." She pushed the papers back into the inside pocket. "It's just that I had my school ID in *my* coat."

The bus rolled to a stop in the heart of the city's refurbished near South Side. Shelby attended a new experimental high school with an emphasis on technology. Their desks were called "hubs." All the students were issued tablets with textbooks loaded digitally. Shelby had expected to attend the high school three blocks away from her home, but her mother had presented a letter saying she had been selected to go the brand new private school with tuition fully paid. She didn't want to go because she was sure Sheila had a hand in her getting accepted to the school.

"Okay, Shelby-Shoe." Mr. Cliff stepped off the back of the bus behind Shelby. "Today's a new day. So, what are you gonna do?"

"Make it do what I want it to!" Shelby retorted. She stood next to Mr. Cliff and liked that she was almost as tall as he was. They high-fived each other and parted ways. Mr. Cliff turned right towards his office in a renovated hotel, and Shelby turned left to her school housed in a refurbished three-story office building.

TELL SHELBY THE TRUTH.

She stuffed Sheila's coat in her locker and headed to the front office. She smelled like Sheila's perfume.

TELL SHELBY THE TRUTH.

"I know what the truth is," Shelby whispered.

The truth was that Sheila was spoiled and hated Shelby. For fifteen years Sheila had gotten all the attention. Shelby's birth had put an end to all that. Was Sheila finally going to come clean? Or was it about their mom? Shelby knew her mother wasn't getting any better.

TELL SHELBY THE TRUTH.

Heat rose in her throat. She thrust the thought aside.

She pushed open the frosted glass door to the office. Ms. Flannery, her guidance counselor, was standing on the other side.

"Why Shelby!" Her southern drawl filled up the room. "I was just coming to look for you." Ms. Flannery had left all her family back in Savannah to come to Chicago to "make a difference."

"Me? I just came down to get a temporary pass. I forgot my ID at home."

Ms. Flannery turned to the woman sitting at the counter. "Lorraine? Can you fix Shelby up with a temporary pass for today? She'll pick it up when we're done."

"Come along, Shelby." Ms. Flannery motioned her towards her office. "Um, that scent is lovely. What is it?"

"I don't know. I have a report due in my first class. I don't want to be late." Shelby hesitated.

"We won't be long. I'll give you a late slip if we are." Ms. Flannery guided Shelby to her office.

"I'm getting all A's and B's in my classes," Shelby assured her.

"I know, and I couldn't be happier with your progress." She pulled out one of the guest chairs and patted the back. Shelby took the seat, and Ms. Flannery sat behind the desk. She turned and looked out the window, then turned back to Shelby. "You know, my window looks right out on your bus stop. I feel like I was given this lovely view to keep a check on you students." She paused. "You know, school started in August. It's now November."

Shelby searched Ms. Flannery's face for some meaning or clarity.

Ms. Flannery continued, "How can I say this? Well, to tell you the truth, Shelby, I was wondering about that man I see you getting off the bus with every day. Is he a relation of yours?"

"Mr. Cliff?" As his name came from Shelby's mouth, Ms. Flannery quickly scrawled it on a yellow pad. "No, I just know him from the bus. Why?"

"So you just meet up as you both are getting off the bus?" Ms. Flannery's Georgia tongue thickened with each question.

"No. Mr. Cliff saves me a seat at the beginning of the line." Shelby watched Ms. Flannery shift in her seat and write on her pad again.

"He seems to dress quite fashionably. Why is he riding the bus?" She leaned forward, wrinkling her nose as if she were talking to one of her twentyish girlfriends.

"I don't know? People ride the bus in Chicago 'cause they don't want to drive." Her heart began to flutter. Ms. Flannery was confusing her.

"True. I have to remember this *is* a big city."

"My mom rode the bus with me on the first day to check the route, and Mr.—" Shelby stopped short of saying his name—"he, was on the bus. He talked with us and told my mama he'd watch out for me." More writing.

"Does he have any children?" Ms. Flannery seemed to force a smile.

"I don't think so. I don't know." The pen scratched against the page. He had just mentioned a niece, but she wouldn't tell Ms. Flannery that.

"Is he married?"

"I don't know. He hasn't said anything." Scribble. Scribble.

Do you have a crush on him? Shelby wanted to ask her.

"Hmm. . . So Shelby, has he ever given you any gifts?"

"No. Just donuts and hot chocolate."

"Donuts and hot chocolate," Ms. Flannery repeated as if confirming facts she already knew.

Shelby didn't dare tell her about the pink hat. Mr. Cliff had given it to her as a souvenir from his ski trip a few months ago.

"Did you tell your mama this man buys you donuts and hot chocolate every morning?"

"No. And it's not every morning." Shelby's voice rose an octave. She took a deep breath and tried to bring it back down. "He's just a nice man who I talk to on the bus."

"Did you tell your mother you sit with him every day?"

"No." They also rode home together on days when Mr. Cliff didn't work late. She was definitely not going to mention that to Ms. Flannery.

"Do you talk about your family?"

Shelby nodded.

Ms. Flannery dropped the pen, and her well-manicured hand gracefully pressed against her forehead.

The heat rose in Shelby's throat again.

"Oh Shelby, does he know yo' daddy passed away and you and yo' momma are alone?" Ms. Flannery's native speech had flourished unabated.

Shelby's heart pounded at high alert in her chest. She thought of all the things she had told Mr. Cliff about her life. How her father hadn't lived to see her graduate eighth grade. How her mother had survived cancer. How now it was back. How her sister was ashamed of their parents and resented her for being born.

"Well, I mean. . ."

"Oh, honey!" Ms. Flannery's delicate hand fell to her chest. Her southern breeding could no longer be contained. "You're out there by yourself. You need to stick with the other kids on the bus. I look out my window every day and see the two of ya getting off that bus slappin' each other five. It is just not proper. There are predators who prey on lonely children."

"Predator! I don't think he—"

8

"Shelby, sometimes the truth is hard to see when you're too close to it."

Ms. Flannery rose from behind the desk and took the seat in the chair opposite Shelby. "I'm gonna have to call your mama about this."

"No! Don't call my house! My mama is sick again. Nothing's going on. He's just somebody on the bus."

"Oh, Shelby. I certainly do not want to worry your mama if she's dealing with health challenges again. It may be something and it may be nothing, but it's my job. I have to report this. High-fives, donuts, hot chocolate, and you're wearing perfume now."

Shelby lowered her head. She was too exhausted to try and explain how she had worn Sheila's overly perfumed coat today. Ms. Flannery probably wouldn't believe her anyway.

Ms. Flannery reached across the desk and squeezed Shelby's hand. "Just know you've done nothing wrong."

"Yes ma'am."

***

Shelby swiped at her tablet, pretending to take notes as Mr. Gordon droned on about geometry. She was actually glad Sheila was picking her up after school today. How could she face Mr. Cliff on the ride home after all Ms. Flannery had said?

As if she had willed her up, Ms. Flannery's face appeared in the glass window of the classroom door. Mr. Gordon opened the door, and they whispered together for a few seconds. She peeked in and gave Shelby a wink and a fluttery wave.

Mr. Gordon closed the door and walked directly to Shelby. He dropped a note on her desk. SISTER UNABLE TO PICK YOU UP. GO STRAIGHT HOME.

Great. It figures, Shelby thought. The one time she wanted Sheila around she didn't keep her promise. Shelby had to make sure she didn't catch the same bus as Mr. Cliff. This probably meant no Chinese Kitchen for dinner either.

***

Shelby pushed through the front door of her house, leaving it standing open behind her. Sheila was waiting in the living room. "So you couldn't pick me up. Why?" Even though Mr. Cliff hadn't been on the bus, her anger still burned at Sheila's broken promise.

"Ms. Flannery called." Sheila stopped short, wringing her hands. "And Mama. . ."

Shelby pulled off the coat and let it fall to the middle of the floor. She found her mother sitting in a lounge chair that seemed to swallow her up, looking more washed out than she had earlier that morning.

"Mama!"

Oxygen tubes now pumped air into her mother's nose. "I'm okay," she whispered through a smile. "I just get a little lightheaded."

Tears filled Shelby's eyes. "That man on the bus—I told Ms. Flannery that nothing was wrong."

"I know," her mother murmured. "Don't blame Ms. Flannery. She's only doing her job."

"She better not have made you sicker!"

"You're getting to be a young lady. You know the cancer's back." She took a few deep breaths. "Ms. Flannery couldn't tell me anything that could make me sicker than I already am. You need to know the truth."

A low moan escaped Shelby as she watched her mother struggle to breathe. "I don't want to." Shelby covered her ears. The last thing she wanted to hear out loud was that her mother was going to die.

"I haven't been honest with you." A coughing spell overtook her.

"*We* haven't been honest with you." Sheila stood behind their mother, holding the coat Shelby had dropped on the living room floor.

Shelby ran over and grabbed the note from the coat pocket.

"Go ahead!" She held the note up to her sister's face. "Here it is! In your own writing! *Tell Shelby the truth!* Well, guess what? Shelby already knows the truth!" She balled the note up and threw it at Sheila. "Just say it out loud!"

Sheila grabbed Shelby in a bear hug. Shelby wiggled to break free, but Sheila only held her tighter.

Tears ran from their mother's eyes and gathered along the oxygen tubes. Shelby faced Sheila with gritted teeth. "Let me go! I want...my...mother!"

"That is not your mother!" Sheila wouldn't let go of her.

Shelby gasped. She felt her heart shudder. Her eyes snapped to the feeble woman sitting in the chair. *Not my mother?* The chair now seemed to dwarf the woman whose mouth was clenched in a tight line as though trying to suppress a wail.

"I'm your mother," Sheila whispered into Shelby's ear. "You are *my* daughter. I've wanted to tell you for years."

Sheila let her go, and Shelby felt her muscles tighten, her nerves throb. She turned to the frail woman sitting in the chair. "Mama?"

"I'm your grandmother, and your dad—he was your grandfather. Don't blame your mother—Sheila. We, your grandfather and I and your father's parents, thought it was best, for everyone involved, to raise you as our daughter."

She paused to catch her breath. "Your parents were teenagers just starting high school. Sheila wanted to tell you when you started going to school, but your grandfather didn't think it was right because we all had agreed. We thought after they finished college, but it was never the right time. Everything got complicated by my cancer, then the accident."

Shelby felt her body convulse as she turned toward Sheila. "You?" Shelby cried. "You don't even care about me?"

"I know you don't think I love you," Sheila said, "but I do. That's why it was hard staying here and not telling you that you were my daughter. Every time you were excited or hurt, you ran to someone else. I had to leave because I wanted to tell you the truth, and they didn't. We fought about it all the time."

Her mother coughed. "Let's not start blaming. It's just important we straighten all this out. With me being sick, we had to tell you."

Shelby sobbed. She felt like she was falling into a deep hole. Sheila put her arms around her.

"Shelby, you are loved. I love you, and your grandma loves you. And your father loves you, but we were so young. This caused problems between your father and me. We tried, but we couldn't stay together and not tell you that you were our child." Sheila hesitated through tears. "He left town, too, but he's back. He's always been supporting you. We both have. Sending Mama and Daddy money to take care of you. He's the one who got you into your school and pays your tuition."

"My father?" The word confused Shelby now. "Who's my father?"

The signature smell of The Chinese Kitchen's shrimp with lobster sauce began to fill the room. Shelby turned towards the aroma.

"Hey, Shelby-Shoe."

Judith Tullis
The Poet and The Pauper

The café table tilts
under the elbows of the poet
dressed in eccentricities:
a muffler of metaphors
around his neck
Pushcart and Pulitzer pinned
to his sonnet-stained coat.

His fingers work
to free the ode stuck in his teeth
while words fall like crumbs
from his beard. A verse trails
unnoticed from the sole of his boot.

In a coat of shabby similes,
the pauper draws near, pleads
"Brother, can you spare a rhyme?

Previously published in *Distilled Lives, Illinois State Poetry Society Anthology*, Infinity Press, 2011

Kevin M. Folliard
Polar Bound

On the morning of December 6th, St. Nicholas Day, ten-year-old twin sisters Alice and Emma awoke to find shimmering gold train tickets in their shoes.

Alice studied her ticket. The front glittered: *Polar Bound Admit 1! Redeemable on Christmas Eve only!* She flipped her ticket and read the fine print aloud:

> *Congratulations! You have been specially chosen for a magical midnight tour of Santa's workshop. At 10PM, once your parents are asleep, please report to the Bell Avenue train stop to board promptly at 10:15. Santa's express train travels through enchanted tunnels, so you will be home with plenty of time to get a good night's rest and spend Christmas Day with your family!*

At the bottom, Santa's perfect signature coiled in silvery pen:

> *Approved by Saint Nicholas.*

The girls were thrilled. Alice wanted to tell their parents, but Emma swore her to secrecy. "If we tell Mom and Dad, they might make us stay home," Emma explained. "They worry too much. And besides, think of all the extra gifts we'll get."

"We already get two of everything," Alice said. "What more could we need?"

Emma sneered. "I'm tired of people treating us like the same person. When I get to the North Pole, I'm marching right up to Santa and demanding that we get different presents from now on.

Alice frowned and nodded. It was true that their parents and grandparents were always buying them identical things. They had the same boots, the same hat and gloves, the same perfect, bobbed blond hair. The same everything. Emma was always complaining about it. But secretly, Alice liked it.

Emma was the smart one. Emma was the friendly one. Everyone loved Emma, and whenever Alice was mistaken for Emma, she took it as the ultimate compliment.

The night before Christmas—once their parents' bedroom light went out across the hall—they waited breathlessly for their father's droning snore. They dressed and snuck down the stairs. Emma had stashed their tickets in their coat pockets before bed. She handed Alice her white parka and fur hat, and they each bundled up.

The Bell Avenue Station was just a few blocks away. Emma twirled her way across the street, her breath clouding around her in a circle. She sang "Santa Claus Is Coming to Town!" Emma's voice was pitch perfect. Alice wondered why she couldn't sing, but her twin sister could.

Confidence, her mother had once told her. *Emma has confidence. That's the only difference.*

As they crossed to the center platform, they spotted other children appearing down the side streets, making their way to the station. Over the next ten minutes, a small crowd of about thirty children gathered. A few of them Alice recognized from school, but nobody she knew personally. She didn't have many friends outside of Emma.

When the town clock struck 10:15PM, the signal lights blinked red, and candy cane colored gates descended. A starry light twinkled on the horizon, shining brighter and brighter.

Steam puffed, wheels clanked, and a high, chipper horn whistled. A chrome green and red engine, decorated with garland, glided along the tracks. An awed hush came over the children as the train slowed and halted. The door of the first passenger car slid open. A tall conductor in a blue and gold uniform leaned out. His green eyes gleamed above a bushy black mustache. "All aboard!"

Alice and Emma waited at the end of the line as the conductor tore tickets. He handed each child a candy cane and tipped his hat as they climbed on. The train's windows glowed warm yellow. The scent of cinnamon wafted outside, accompanied by the soft echo of "Jingle Bell Rock."

Alice's heart pulsed with excitement. Emma's lips were pursed tight. She glared up and down the line of children.

"Can you believe this?" Alice whispered. She squeezed the puffy white arm of her sister's coat.

Emma twisted away. "Yes, I can. Calm down."

"Emma, we're going to the North Pole!"

"Shh!" Emma put a gloved finger to her lips and narrowed her eyes. "I know what's going on. Keep quiet."

"Why?"

Emma huffed. She stood tip-toed to see over the line. "What's taking so long?"

"Just be patient," Alice whispered.

As they drew closer, the line stopped moving for a few minutes. A second conductor arrived to help a boy in a wheelchair onto the train.

"Why would they let a handicapped boy on?" Emma groaned. "They just slow things down."

"Maybe he's been a really good boy," Alice said. "That's all Santa cares about."

Emma grew silent.

The girls reached the front of the line. The conductor smiled at Emma. He glanced at her ticket and tore it. Pixie dust glittered to the ground. "All aboard, young lady!" He handed her a candy cane.

Emma hurried onto the train and disappeared to the left.

Alice retrieved her ticket from her front coat pocket and handed it to the conductor. He took a look at it and frowned. "I'm sorry, miss! No admission."

Alice stared incredulously. "What? It's the same ticket!"

"I'm afraid not." The conductor pointed to a red asterisk on the front of her ticket. He turned it around and showed her the signature at the bottom: *Lord Atnas.*

He lowered his voice. "That's the southbound train."

Alice shook her head in refusal. "No! I'm on *this* train. That was my sister."

The conductor sighed. "Your sister *is* on this train." He took out a gold cellphone and scanned her ticket's barcode. "Says here you like to manipulate your sister. You lie to your parents and teachers, and you cheated on a math test."

"That was Emma!"

The conductor took her by the arm. He found a tag on the interior of her coat sleeve and scanned it. "This is your coat, Emma. Santa gave it to you last year."

"Emma took my coat! Please, this is a mistake!"

The conductor shook his head and gestured to his cell phone. "I'm sorry, but the naughty list profile is flagged for fibbing. Step aside. Give my regards to Father Whip."

A clap of thunder shook the air as an oily black train screeched along the southbound track. Metal thorns rimmed the wheels. Thick, iron bars crossed the passenger windows, and a silver skull adorned the cattle catcher.

Emma sat in the window of the northbound train, sipping cocoa. She laughed at something across the aisle. Alice screamed, but her sister didn't seem to hear.

The black train squealed to a halt. Iron gates scraped open. Both trains blocked the exits. The conductor of the northbound train tipped his hat and prepared to shut the door. Alice grabbed his coat. "Please! Tell my sister that I'm out here!"

He brushed her away. "I don't make exceptions for non-ticket holders. If you have a problem, take it up with the southbound conductor." The emerald door slid shut.

From the black train, a burly, ten-foot troll ducked out onto the platform. White scabs and mossy fungus speckled his green skin. His scarred, hog-like face sneered. An iron ring hung from his upturned nose. His voice erupted, dark and fiery like molten steel: "South Pole! Get in!"

The monster beckoned Alice with a clawed finger. "Don't make me ask twice, maggot!"

Alice caught one final glimpse of her sister in the warm yellow window. Emma smiled and waved goodbye as the shimmering chrome engine chugged north.

The monster snatched Alice by the shoulder. She screamed. His hot, foul breath steamed over her face. "No use struggling, kid! Nobody gets out of this. Read the fine print!"

Alice shouted and pleaded. She twisted uselessly, but the conductor's iron grip held her in place. "You can't make me go! You can't!"

"Maybe not this year! But sooner or later Father Whip catches up to you. Just come get it over with, brat! It's not so bad when you're young."

Alice stopped struggling. "What do you mean?"

"I mean read the *fine print*!" He snatched the ticket away and held it in front of her eyes. "In the spirit of the season, tickets may be refused in lieu of an extended summer stay."

"Summer?"

"Yeah! Father Whip's Antarctic Summer Camp. Lasts three weeks instead of just the one night. Now get on! No one wants that!" He started to drag her.

"I do," Alice said.

"What!"

"I want to go to the South Pole this summer instead of tonight," she said louder.

The conductor sneered. A tiny black bug crawled between his teeth. He gave a low, grating laugh of dark delight. "You have no idea what you just agreed to." He released her arm and pocketed the ticket.

"Yes, I do." Alice smiled. "I need to learn my lesson well, so that someday, I might become a better person. Like my sister Alice."

Lorelei Glaser
Mea Culpa

Her two-hour hair treatment finished, Annie could finally leave the salon. She looked away from the large, square windows that framed rumbling freight and passenger trains on their inexorable journeys.

Stiff and tired, she pulled herself out from the leather padded swivel chair. The salon's chairs were reputed to be ergonomically designed. *Really?*

Annie glanced at herself in the mirror. Lips curled in a coquettish smile, she mused, "Nothing like a fresh hairdo."

With small, careful steps, she walked toward the coat room, hoping no one would notice the tell-tale gait of fear and pain. *Don't fall*, she scolded herself. Had it been four years since the surgery—since cadavers shared their vertebrae with her? She remembered laughing at a TV commercial years ago—an old woman struggling on her kitchen floor, reaching out, crying, "I've fallen, and I can't get up!"

At last, without falling, she reached the coat room. She rummaged through the clump of coats and jackets hanging on a rack. *Are women's coats all black, navy blue—all from REI, The North Face? All with a variety of pockets, hoods and zippers?*

This is mine, thought Annie. She lifted the coat from the rack, pushed her arms through the sleeves. Annie motioned good bye to customers and stylists and left the salon, door chimes signaling her departure.

Shivering, she lifted the coat collar around her neck. The temperature had dropped steadily during the afternoon. A sharp wind caught wisps of her hair. Only 4:00PM, the sky was already dark.

Annie walked toward her black, VW Rabbit, fumbled through a bulky purse. With a sigh of relief, she grasped the car keys. It was always comforting to find her keys. She'd been so absent-minded lately.

Driving home, she worried: *had she left a tip for the beautician?* "Oh well," she murmured. "Maybe next time—if I remember."

Annie gripped the steering wheel, made a sharp left turn. *Why,* she wondered, *is it so awkward to move my arm, to turn the steering wheel? Why are the sleeves so tight?* She pulled into a grocery store parking lot, quickly got out of the car. She tugged her arms out of the sleeves, pulled off the coat.

The wrong coat.

Navy blue, REI, but not her coat.

Except for the narrow sleeves, Annie thought, *I like the way this coat fits...more stylish than mine. If I don't wear a heavy sweat shirt underneath, the sleeves won't be so tight. I suppose the owner will soon know her coat is missing. What to do?*

Annie laughed at herself. She slid her hands into the warm pockets of the coat.

In the right pocket, her fingers felt a tissue. *Of course. Everyone has tissue in their coat pockets to wipe teary eyes on cold, windy days.* And today was both cold and windy.

But what else? A piece of paper?

In the left pocket, her fingers circled a small piece of white note paper, folded twice. She unfolded it and saw thin pen strokes:

So sorry. I can't go on any longer. Please forgive me.

Annie froze, her feet riveted to the concrete, fingers clenched around the small piece of paper.

Wait, she thought.

No. Don't wait. Do something. Go back to the salon. Find the coat's owner.

For warmth, Annie eased into the coat, slid back into the car. *Did I really consider keeping this coat?* Dreamlike, the question circled through her mind. She jammed the note back into the coat pocket, pressed her foot down hard on the accelerator.

Go faster, hurry.

She approached a train crossing. "Please," she murmured. "Stay up, gates. Stay away, train. Wait until I've crossed." She gritted her teeth, drove faster.

These damn suburbs and their countless configurations of tracks and trains.

Annie saw men and women running toward her car, waving their arms, faces distorted, mouths opening and closing. Was there a problem?

Bells clanged. Flashing red lights in the distance, a myriad of red and white stripes. . .

Penitence. Yes.

Mea culpa.

Too late.

Linda Lea Graziani
Fifi and Madame

CHARACTERS
FIFI: a young, fluffy, white poodle.
MADAME: a mature, bright pink poodle.
LADY: the rich owner of the dogs.

SCENE:
*The glamorous living room of a penthouse overlooking the Eiffel
Tower in Paris.*

MADAME: *(Peering down to the busy street below.)* That takes
the cake. It is only September and every master has already
dressed their better halves in the new fall couture coats!
FIFI: *(Curling up on a chaise lounge.)* You have been pacing back
and forth in front of the window all morning. What on earth
could be bothering you?
MADAME: Ha! Don't you dare act so innocent with moi.
FIFI: How would I know what you are raving about?
MADAME: Oh, I want to see it again. Lady told me it was so
special that I would only be wearing it on beautiful sunny days
like this.
FIFI: Wear what, Madame? You have a whole closet full of clothes.
MADAME: You dumb pup. Of course, it is my Vivienne Westwood
diamond coat. 4,000 Euros down the toilet.
FIFI: Oh, now I remember. Lady came back from her London
shopping trip and brought you the sparkling diamond coat.

Do you remember my sparkling gift? A plaid collar. Well that was fair, wasn't it? Plaid. As if!

MADAME: Lady and I are well aware of how fair you thought that was. When we returned from our debut promenade with the diamond coat, you had ripped up half of my new winter clothes. (*Raising her voice.*) You behaved like an unsophisticated mutt. There, it had to be said. And I am not sorry!

FIFI: (*Loudly.*) I was bought by Lady because you are too old for her to have fun with. You embarrass her—with your useless bladder—having to be walked five times a day. Mon Dieu!

MADAME: And to think I welcomed you into my home. Oh là là! My Lady will soon tire of your bizarre behavior. Good riddance I say. But tell me, before she throws you and your hideous plaid collar out, what have you done to my wonderful coat?

FIFI: (*Leaving the room.*) Wouldn't you like to know? Au revoir. I have had enough of your senile rants.

MADAME: Do you dare turn your back on your leader?

FIFI: You are not my leader. You pink puff ball! And you really do look ridiculous in that coat. I, however, would look magnifique. My Lady will see that soon enough.

MADAME: Your Lady! Enfant terrible! I have been with her for 15 years. You are nothing to her. Why do you think you did not get a couture coat? I would rather not resort to this, but if you do not bring moi the coat this minute, I will be forced to tell my Lady who piddled on her new comforter.

FIFI: How dare you, you old bag of bones! Lady gave me too much champagne. I was tipsy. Big deal.

MADAME: Well, I'll leave it up to you. But I am not sure if Lady will forgive your mutt-like behavior. We are a class better than you. You must improve or you will be out on the street.

FIFI: Mon Dieu, I hate you. (*She trots into the kitchen. A door squeaks. Fifi returns to the living room carrying the missing coat in her teeth and drops it.*) Here is your ratty diamond thing. I hope the diamonds are so heavy that they break your tiny frail legs.

MADAME: (*She walks over to the coat.*) Oh, my chic coat! Finally out of your evil mongrel clutches. But why is it so dirty?

FIFI: (*Laughing.*) It has gotten old and rotten like you. Now you both match. (*Fifi prances triumphantly away.*)

LADY: (*Lady energetically bursts through the front door swinging a gold gift bag.*) Bonjour, my babies. Oh, Madame, why do you look so sad? Mon Dieu! What happened to your new coat? Fifi! Come here you bad thing! (*Fifi cautiously walks in the room with her tail between her legs.*) Oh, not again my baby. This can't keep happening. I spend too much money on Madame's clothes to have them ripped apart or dirtied every time I turn my back.

MADAME: (*In a whisper.*) Now you are going to get it. Adieu, Fifi!

LADY: (*She reaches into her bag and pulls out another diamond coat.*) I wasn't fair to my precious Fifi, was I? Both my girls must have the best outfits in France. Look what I have for you, Fifi.

FIFI: Mon Dieu! My lady does love me! Oh, I don't deserve it.

MADAME: No, you don't. You have been too jealous of my joie de vivre.

LADY: Of course, Madame will receive the new diamond coat. And Fifi, you will wear the one you tried to destroy. That is only fair, right, ma chérie?

MADAME: Oui, that is right. I get the brand new coat for all of the trouble I have had to endure with that mutt.

FIFI: You really love me? Lady, I will gratefully wear the dirty diamonds. Dirty diamonds are better than a new plaid collar any day. Oh là là!

Judith Kessler
Coat Thief

Having finished with her work at the Botanic Gardens, Marilyn picks up her coat at the membership desk. Deciding to take a quick look at the autumn array, she strolls over the bridge to the gardens. The sun is just beginning its descent.

She frowns as she puts on her coat. Something's wrong. The coat feels too roomy. It's too long. The color's right, but the buttons are a little bigger. And what's this? A few pet hairs that don't belong! Ah! Bulging pockets! Definitely not her coat! In the pockets, something jingles. Coins? No! Mercedes car keys!

She hears footsteps behind her. A clean-shaven, well-dressed man appears. A coat is draped over his arm.

HE: Wow, what luck! Marilyn? Dartmouth 2005?

SHE: David? Dartmouth 2004? And is that *my* coat you're carrying?

HE: I'm sorry. I must've grabbed your coat by mistake! But say, you look fetching in *my* coat raking the ground.

SHE: Yes, gardener for hire." *She curtsies.* "I remember you saved me in Chem 101.

HE: Yes, it's fortunate no one got hurt. Our Tech Writing class wasn't my forte. You saved me there. You married Fred?

SHE: He's history. What about Olivia?

HE: We didn't make it to the altar . . . A good thing . . . How about we share dinner?

SHE: Me with a coat thief?

HE: Your coat is my stunning arm piece.

SHE: Yes, of course, the charming thief. (*She smiles.*)

HE: Over dinner, I might persuade you of my finer qualities. Our wrong coats might become a good fit.

SHE: Well, David, (*she takes his arm*), I believe that all depends on the quality of the material.

HE: Hmm, quality of the material, huh? I suppose I could try to finagle myself out of this one. It just might take more than fast food at McDonald's. How much change do we have in my coat pocket?

Janet Barrett
Pocketful

My hand in your pocket,
yours in mine.
Yet, neither of us in between.

Who picked up my coat?
What did I acquire?
To whom should I aspire?

Pocketful of posies, sealed in a card,
one petal short.
The card had shifted.
Out tiny holes, sooty remains sifted.

A flower pressed, nonetheless,
now, through my fingers,
imagination's peat.

Pocketful of posies
brings to mind the rosies. . .
Red, grey-rosed faces,
pale, pallid pallor.

Plagued!
Left aghast, lying prone,
grimaces cast upon a stone.

What could be at stake with that one missing flake?
Rogue DNA, gone astray,
could signify a world's generation, fey.

'Scuse me,
I think I've got your dance card.
Pardon me, my mistake.
Your coat, I did not purposely take.

My coat pocket held but
two lint pieces and a quarter.

What I got into remains unknown.
A smudge on a headstone. . .
mine now?
Let's hope it doesn't linger atop my finger.

Jim Chmura
Best in Plaid

"But you just can't leave him like that!" my older sister shouted at me.

We were in Parlor #3 of the Evermore Funeral Home. My twin brother lay in his casket, arms folded on his chest. He was looking good in a crisp white shirt, natty red necktie, and navy blue sports coat. Eleanor and I were viewing his mortal remains prior to regular visiting hours. It was as if we were supposed to inspect him and sign off that all was okay. Apparently all was not okay.

She pointed at Adam. I shrugged.

"That is *not* the coat he wanted to be buried in. That is the *wrong* coat. He was very specific about that plaid sports jacket." She poked me in the chest. "And look, this blue coat has a large stain on its right lapel." She shook her head. "How could you?"

"A funeral is for the living, not the deceased." I studied Adam for a moment. "He is very, very deceased."

I didn't tell her that his last wheeze was "plaid." Or was it "please?" No matter. Maybe he was willing me his wonderful plaid coat. Maybe he was full of remorse for a life squandered. Maybe he really wanted to be buried in the plaid coat. I didn't really care because now it was mine.

"You're a real bastard. Where you got the gall to wear his coat to his wake is beyond me."

"Come on, Eleanor, I deserve this coat. I put up with his crap for years. He was one lazy bastard. After he got this coat, he always had shit luck—a lady on his arm, a buck in his pocket, and a smile on his face. He never, ever shared." I brushed a sleeve. "Who knows, maybe it was the coat. Maybe it has some kinda spell from that weird resale shop where he bought it."

"It sure wasn't those colors," she said. "So why didn't you see if they had another one?"

"Couldn't. The joint mysteriously burned down before I could get over there. They never did find the owners."

***

Adam was duly processed and went to his eternal reward in the navy blue sports coat, stain and all. From that day forward, I would be able to wear the plaid coat. He'd never given in even when I begged. Not once. You'd think 65-year-old twins would act more mature.

Adam and me had been living in the family home. I dumped it as quick as I could and moved into a downtown condo. The only family left was a few distant cousins. Unlike Adam, I was pretty shy, but I decided to make the best of whatever came my way.

***

"My, that is snazzy," said the handsome lady in the condo elevator. I nodded and straightened the lapels. "You're new here, aren't you?" She touched my sleeve. That was the first encounter in my new world of the plaid coat. Soon I was gently folding and setting it down by her bedside.

***

"Hey you!" a man called as I strolled by the movie set on Monroe Street. "You with that plaid job, wanna be an extra?" That was good for about six weeks of walking behind the legendary Hollywood star, Edgar Loudgear. I played his therapist in his newest conspiracy film *Someone is Bad*. I had a small part, but fans treated me like a star because of my proximity to Mr. Loudgear.

"Might get me one of those plaid jobs someday," Loudgear said as he patted my shoulder on the final day of shooting.

The following day, during the evening rush hour, a taxicab screeched to a halt a few inches from me and a mother with her child. "Goddamnit," the cabby swore. "If it weren't for that loud ass coat, you and the lady would've been mooshed."

In gratitude, her husband wrote me a very nice check.

The next morning as I walked along Wabash, shots rang out. An evildoer dashed from the bank right in front of me. My bright plaid distracted him for a nano-second, just enough for the pursuing officer to gronk him on the head with a billy club.

My picture appeared on page one of the *Trib*, above the fold no less.

I would wait for the plaid while it was being cleaned and pressed at ChiChang's 30-Minute Cleaners. "You no have to wait," ChiChang said. "But I must," I insisted. I tipped him heavily to ensure quality handling.

***

Early October, one year after Adam's death, I went to the cemetery. This was to be my final visit and farewell. I was feeling brazen, so I wore his plaid. I paid the cab driver, told him to wait, and walked up the slope to Adam's grave. It was getting late and a bit clammy. I bowed my head to pray for his desolate soul.

A sudden damp wind blew leaves and twigs from his grave against my legs. I shivered and pulled the coat tight around me. Twins are supposed to communicate without speaking. We never did during life, but my dear brother sure seemed to be giving it a shot now.

"I get the message, Adam," I said. I slowly slipped off the plaid and started to set it on his tombstone. Then I paused and shook it over his grave. "Take a good long look, you bastard, because this is the last time either the coat or I will be here."

I put it on, brushed off the lapels, and strode down the slope. The idiot cab was gone. I looked around for a ride. Nobody but the dead. I swallowed hard and started to hustle along the cemetery road. I felt like the tombstones were staring at me so I shortcut between some graves, stumbled, and tore the elbow of the coat. By time I reached the main gate, it was near dark, cold and windy. I was sweating like a hog.

"Unless you sleep here," Mr. ChiChang said the next morning, "you cannot wait for coat. Must get right color threads to fix nice. Come back next Tuesday."

I moaned. "But that's a whole week!"

Mr. Chichang nodded. He walked to the back of his shop and returned with a very ugly brown sport coat. "You try this," he said.

I did.

"Busy tonight." The handsome lady in the elevator sneered.

***

Edgar Loudgear was back in town for opening night of *Someone is Bad*. I had forced my way to the front of frantic fans outside the

Bellows Theater for the grand premier. I figured Loudgear would catch a glimpse of me. He cruised by, nodding and smiling. He didn't even blink when he passed right in front of me.

As I ambled home, a Smash Cab splashed through a puddle. The cold, muddy soup soaked a nearby lady and me.

"You moron," the lady screeched. "That car almost hit me because of you."

I slunk away.

I had only gone two blocks when I was stopped by a short, fat thug. A scraggily mustache covered his mouth. "Hey, Wet and Ugly," he growled. "Wallet and watch and you ain't gonna get hurt."

"Here, take the coat," I said after I handed over my watch and wallet. "You took everything else."

"That?" He snickered. "You gotta be kiddin'."

I cowered inside the rest of the week, now convinced that the mysterious plaid was my key to success and happiness.

***

"Perfect!" I said as I tipped Mr. ChiChang a twenty on Tuesday morning.

"Is very special material," ChiChang said. "Where you get coat?"

"A family heirloom," I said. I checked the sleeve.

"You want to sell?"

"Never!"

Wednesday, I proudly strutted onto the elevator wearing the plaid.

"Hey big boy, where you been?" that handsome lady asked. Life was good.

Thursday, a Smash Cab gave me a free ride because I was his 1,000th customer.

Friday, I sported the plaid to lunch at Earl's Deli, a local haunt of the rich and famous. I was about to take a bite of my corned beef sandwich when Edgar Loudgear slapped me on the back.

"Nice to see you," he said. "How 'bout I join you?"

Sunday, I prayed at church with the plaid. I even murmured a few lines on my brother's behalf. As I walked outside, I bumped into that moustache thug. He paused and glared at me. He touched the coat.

"I'm sorry," he blurted.

"Oh ye sinner," I said in my best preachy tone.

With tears in his eyes, he handed me my watch and wallet.
I left him with Pastor Beels and redemption.

***

The email said Halloween Family Reunion at Cousin Zelda's.
"Yuck!" I said. I hadn't seen that dizzy dame in years.
"Would be fun," that handsome lady said when I told her. She winked and tapped the elevator STOP button. Life was very good.

***

We went. She was a sexy vampire. I just wore the plaid. It was enough.

The party was big, really big. We danced to the live music and laughed. Some guy about my size started to lurk around. She smiled at his hideous skull mask. He brought me one, two and then three Zombies, each one a bit stronger. I wondered how he knew I loved those damned drinks. My date, the handsome lady, tenderly held the last one to my lips until the glass was empty. I became woozy, and leaned against a wall. I wiped sweat from my brow.

"Here," the handsome lady said over her cleavage. "Let me make you more comfortable."

I panted as I stared down her slinky gown while she gently slid the coat off my shoulders.

"That's perfect," she cooed. She left me and set it on a pile of coats near the door.

One her way back to me, Hideous Skull Mask touched her arm. I tried to speak but slurred my words. She left to do another Boogaloo with him. After a bit, I couldn't see my date and wasn't feeling all too good. So I decided to leave alone. I ransacked the pile of coats at the door, but no plaid sports coat!

I slouched next to Cousin Zelda, watching as partygoers bid her adieu. Nobody was wearing my coat. It was gone!

"My plaid sports coat," I moaned. "Did you see it?"

"Of course," Zelda mumbled, giving me an unwanted squeeze. She was in worse shape than me. "Who could miss those colors? I was thrilled to see you again! I haven't heard a word about you boys in twenty years."

"Boys?" I pushed away. "What boys?"

"Why you and Adam of course."

"But Adam is . . ."

"Yes, yes, wearing that ugly mask." She tapped her finger against her cheek. "At least I think it was Adam. He actually looked like a dead version of you." She belched. "Anyhooow, whoever he is, left with that loud plaid coat and your date on his arm. You boys were always so competitive."

Zelda reached for the only remaining coat. "You may as well take this one."

As she lifted the coat, something tumbled from its folds to the floor—the ugly skull mask. Zelda held the coat up for me to slip on. I blinked. Rubbed my eyes. Blinked again. But the coat didn't change.

It was navy blue with a big stain on the right lapel.

Joan Nelson
Mistake

I picked up a coat
That looked like mine;
But the sleeves were too short,
Though the shoulders fit fine.

The color was black and
The pockets just right;
But a button was missing,
And the arms were too tight.

I reached in the pocket
And pulled out some keys;
Found a perfumed linen hanky
That brought on a sneeze.

The opposite pocket held only a hole;
'Twas in the lining that went far below.
An object in the hem
Took me by surprise.

I pulled it upward;
It was an elegant size.
A huge diamond ring captured the light,
Sparkles and glitters blinded my sight.

'Twas a Tiffany gem!
Keep it? Return it? But then,
A tap on my shoulder gave me a fright.
A woman told me, "Something's not right.

"Let's switch coats, and then you'll see,
This one fits you because that diamond fits me."

Ruth Princess
The Michelin Man

The view from my 4th floor dorm window was a giant barren oak tree, and across the street a four-story parking garage. Clearly visible on the top deck of the garage was my family's old 1971 Grand Safari station wagon with a clamshell tailgate and back facing seats. I called him Sherman the Power Tank.

Everyone knew his name because I'd taken white house paint and scrawled it across the rust-speckled army green finish.

One Monday morning in January, my clock radio woke me with a list of school closings. I covered my head with my comforter and curled into a tight ball. The announcer warned that it wasn't only the rapidly accumulating snow causing the closings.

"Last night's freezing rain and 50-mile-per-hour sustained winds left a two to three inch coating of ice everywhere. Electric crews are going to have trouble repairing downed lines with the predicted two feet of snow followed by plummeting temperatures in the next 24 hours."

Three hours later, I woke again and crawled out of bed. The earlier announcement hadn't prepared me for the sight out the window. Arctic air loomed like fog in a haunted house. The oak tree had been transformed into a shiny black monster frozen in mid grip, reaching out as if to strangle little children passing underneath. Clear glass spikes protruded from the branches like a dinosaur's protective mane.

Snow accumulated on the ground, but the tree's slick, oddly angled icicles and drooping branches couldn't hold the white powder. Across the street, snow swirled on the garage deck like a giant white tornado.

I grabbed the last morsel of food from the mini fridge and crawled back in bed.

The next day, I awoke to bright sunshine intensified by reflective snow. I couldn't hole up all day again; I was out of food.

I looked out the window. The tree monster was still frozen. The white cement garage had grown an igloo fifth story. Sherman, buried under the snow, was nowhere to be seen.

I put on jeans, a turtleneck, sweatshirt, and ratty black boots. Next, I had to decide between my long white puffy coat or my cute little ski jacket.

My dad had given me the long white coat for Christmas two years ago. He'd taken me on a weekend trip to Chicago. It was so cold that we stopped into an expensive store on the Magnificent Mile where he bought the coat for me. The coat was warm, practical, and comforting, just like my dad. The coat was special to me.

"You look like the Michelin Man," is what my ex-boyfriend had said the first time he saw me in it. I didn't like how I looked in it either, but when I wore it, it was like getting a hug from my dad.

But on campus, I dreaded guys seeing me in the white puffy coat looking like the Michelin Man. Well, I'd be driving not walking today. I didn't need warm, practical, and comforting.

I donned the cute little ski jacket.

As soon as I opened my door, a floor mate asked if I was going to the store. Most dorm people didn't have cars on campus. I took her list and some money.

Down the hall, I heard a terrible barking. I poked my head in a doorway. "Helga, you sound terrible. Can I get you anything?"

"Please," she struggled to whisper. "My doctor called in a prescription. Can you go to the drug store?"

Downstairs in the lobby, suave Steve greeted me.

"You look so good in that ski jacket."

"Thanks! You said that Saturday at Dan's party, but you were probably too drunk to remember."

"I was also too drunk to remember my hat and gloves. Would you mind stopping by Dan's and picking them up for me?"

"Sure, I've got a ton of errands to run, what's one more?"

Steve's smile warmed me on the inside. I put on my own hat and gloves to face the cold outside.

I opened the carved wood front door and squinted at the noontime glare. I entered a three-by-three-foot icicle jail. Apparently, I wasn't the only one who had been holing up inside. I broke two stalactites to reach the sidewalk.

I crossed the plowed street and climbed to the top of the parking garage. I wasn't sure if I could get my tank to plow through the waist-high snow. I trudged along, sliding my feet and pushing the snow with my legs. I was working up a sweat.

I'm glad I didn't grab my old Michelin Man puffy coat.

Sherman hid in a six-foot snowdrift. *What good is a snowbrush on the inside of a car?*

I burrowed through snow until I reached my green metal heap. I brushed snow from the driver's side window and down to the door handle. The window didn't seem to stop. A clear sheet of ice covered the car deeper than the depth of the handle.

I chiseled ice with the car key.

Chip, chip, chip.

I danced a little as the cold ground crept through my boots. I chiseled harder and faster. A sweat broke out on my forehead.

Will my car even start?

Chip, chip, chip.

Would a hot pot stay hot enough to melt the ice? The icy wind howled. *If the rain had frozen at 45° angles from the wind, this subzero chill factor would make the old trick of pouring water on a lock worse, not better.*

Chip, chip, chip.

Success! I jammed the key into the lock and turned. Click.

I lifted the handle and pulled. Nothing happened. I brushed away more snow. Ice had sealed the doors shut.

Chip, chip, chip.

The snowdrift blew on me. Snow covered my back. Cold numbed my toes. I grabbed my tattered ski lift tag, partially unzipped my jacket, and wiped my brow. I lifted the door handle and tugged.

CRACK!

The door flew open. I landed butt first in a snow bank.

I wiped snow from my soggy jeans and crawled into the car. The vinyl seat crackled under my weight. At least now I was sheltered from the wind. I shut the door and put the key in the ignition.

I crossed my fingers. "Please start. Please start. Sherman, be good to me."

I closed my eyes and turned the key. Rrrr, clunk.

"Come on Sherman. You can do it."

Rrrr, rrrr, clug, clug, brr-roooom.

"Yes! You're my power tank." I patted the dashboard.

I cranked up the heat. Cold air blasted my face. I turned off the fan and prayed for heat soon.

Sherman growled forward, spraying snow away from his wheels like he was Moses parting the Red Sea. Sherman slid like he was competing in a game of Atari racecar on ice, circling down the parking garage. When we hit the salted, plowed street, it was smooth sailing.

The drug store was a mile away. Another mile later, I stopped at my part-time job to pick up my paycheck. Next stop, I popped into the bank to cash my check. Another mile away was the party house where I picked up Steve's hat and gloves. Each time I got in the car, the seat would crunch and I'd crank the heat only to be blasted by cold.

I looked at the dashboard and added another stop to my list. I needed gas just to get to the grocery store. Pumping five dollars-worth of gas in a car that only gets six miles to the gallon wasn't much. But I couldn't endure the cold through my gloves as I held the nozzle and hopped on frozen feet.

As I drove the five miles to the grocery store, snow billowed through the hole of the rusted floorboard to the left of the brake pedal. I wiggled my toes.

When I came out of the store, it was already dark. I didn't think I'd been in there that long, since I still hadn't warmed up. The analog clock in the car indicated that dinner in the dorm was in 30 minutes. My dinners were prepaid, and I couldn't afford to eat my groceries as meals.

I drove home, dropped off everyone's stuff. I didn't even take off my coat before jumping in line for dinner.

***

"Hi Margo. How was Medical class?"

"Too cold for even me to go. The professor said class was optional today. Why did you go out? Your face looks wind burned."

"I had to run a bunch of errands. I want to eat quickly and then take a hot shower. I can't even feel my toes." Although the floor was not ice cold like the pavement, I was still dancing.

Margo grabbed her tray and handed me one. It immediately dropped to the ground.

"I'm sorry. I guess my fingers are still numb."

Our choice for dinner was Chicken Tetrazzini or Tuna Surprise. We chose the lesser of two evils and plopped down at a table with friends.

As my friends cheerily chatted, I rubbed my feet together and squirmed in my seat. When I accidentally dropped my fork, Margo turned to me. "Are you OK? You're awfully quiet tonight."

"My hands and feet itch so bad. It's driving me crazy."

"How long were you outside? You might have frostbite."

Margo looked at my blue fingers, grabbed me by the arm and rushed me upstairs.

She gently applied a warm washcloth to my hands in the hall bathroom. Eventually we ran warm water over my tingling fingers. When the pain subsided, Margo took off my boots. "These are soaking wet!" she exclaimed.

The tile floor was cold, so Margo threw a towel down for me to stand on. She hoisted my leg to the sink. When the one foot was taken care of, she worked on the other.

"If you'd waited another half hour, I bet you'd be in the health center. You should be fine now."

"Thank you, Margo. I'm so glad you're pre-med. I'm ready to take my coat off and take a hot shower."

"Not too hot! You don't want to damage your tender skin."

I grabbed my boots and went to my room. I slowly undressed, shivering as I removed each layer, pausing in between to adjust to the new temperature. I eventually stripped down and curled up in my robe under my comforter. When I felt a little warmer, I slipped into my flip-flops and headed back to the bathroom with my shower bucket and towel. I turned on the shower and tested the temperature with my hand. It felt hot but not painful. I hung up my robe and stepped inside the stall.

The water rushed down my front, and I just stood there breathing deeply. It was the first time I felt warm since Steve smiled at me. I sang, "Oh the weather outside is frightful, but the snow is so delightful. And since we've no place to go, let it snow, let it snow, let it snow."

I increased the temperature and wished there was a fireplace in the dorms. I turned to warm my butt in the water.

"Arrggg! Margo, help!" I shut the water off.

No response from Margo or anyone else.

I leaped out of the shower and rushed naked to the mirror. I examined my backside through the reflection. My prickly butt was a deep dark purple.

Oh boy, I thought. *I think I grabbed the wrong coat this morning.*

I flung on my robe and hurried back to my dorm room. I knew just what I needed right now.

A hug from the Michelin Man.

Coat Check

Finally, Maddie Silk could sit.

That Steak Place was full. The restaurant's next scheduled seating was sixty minutes away. Maddie would have no more coats to check for a while. There'd be a reprieve from the icy wind that whipped in snow and shivers whenever Quentrell the doorman opened the thick glass door.

In a typical night, she would hang nearly half-a-million-dollars' worth of coats. Tonight, she had already taken a Berluti Quilted Leather Jacket (msrp $9,150) from a dapper old dandelion head (her term for the puffy white afro that rich old white guys thought was in right now); a Dennis Basso Chinchilla and Suede Overcoat (msrp $14,396) from the dandelion head's studly young companion; and several designer mink fur coats that likely topped $20K each.

Maddie began googling the furs on her phone. Damn, she was chilled. One of those furs would warm her fast. She'd never worn fur. Never would. She'd freeze before she'd wear fur. But as long as Quentrell didn't open the door for a while, she wouldn't freeze.

Quentrell was technically not a doorman. He supervised a team of three parking attendants. He only parked cars during the rush. The rest of the time he preferred to stand regally by the door and play doorman.

Doormen and valet parking attendants could dress for brutal Chicago winters. Maddie, stationed near the entrance, had to wear a white shirt that showed plenty of cleavage, a black pencil skirt that showed plenty of leg, and blood red heels no one could see unless they leaned over the coat check counter and watched her hang or retrieve their coats.

She was pretty sure nobody watched. To the customers, she was just part of the invisible infrastructure supporting the dining delights they deserved.

Maddie's cell phone chirped. A text from Quentrell. A joke.

Only thing doormen like bout rich fulks is their money.

Nothing from Lester.

She sighed, texted *luv u missing u* to Lester, and then texted Quentrell: *Thx for the typo!! U given me a polite way to F-Bomb the next bad tipper!*

He texted right back.

Hope u know typo was consonant not vowel.

She laughed, texted a smile, then began whispering to herself.

"Hope you fulks enjoyed your meal. Hope you fulks enjoyed your meal."

She kept repeating it until she was satisfied she'd weakened the long OH sound in folks just enough to make them wonder. Maybe they'd frown, but she'd give them her cheek-dimpling smile.

Anyway, Lester would take her side if there were any complaints.

She rolled on her stool to her tip jar. Despite management's rule that the tip jar should be at the end of the counter, she'd placed it right in the middle, so nobody—no *rich fulks*—could pretend they didn't see it.

She grabbed the tip jar and knelt before a plastic bin under the counter. The bin held her stuff: boots (L.L. Bean), tote bag (Longchamp), hat (hand knitted with her own hands in crazy expensive alpaca wool), coat (Burberry). She worked in a closet but management required her to put her stuff in a plastic bin on the floor. God forbid her coat hang next to a customer's.

She opened her tote and poured in the contents of the tip jar. Wrinkled bills spilled out. A wrapped condom. A baggie of white powder (probably baking soda). And a poker chip. A five-dollar chip from the Venetian in Las Vegas.

A poker chip? What was that all about?

Vegas was what, two thousand miles away from Chicago?

Vegas was where Lester had promised to take her when she turned 21, but she'd turned 21 three months ago. What he'd given her instead of a Vegas vacay was a blackplum-colored Burberry London Cashmere Trench Coat which retailed for $1396 at Nordstrom.

But he hadn't exactly bought it at Nordstrom.

She'd learned, when she'd tried to exchange it, that he'd actually gotten the coat for $299.99 (final sale, no returns, no exchanges) at Nordstrom Rack, there being a small stain in the inner lining, a nearly invisible quarter-inch rip in the right sleeve, and imperfectly aligned gold domed buttons (for a military vibe) which did not line up in two perfect vertical rows.

She dug in her bag, found the poker chip, and tossed it over the counter. It bounced against the opposite wall, then settled on the floor near a glass table holding a huge arrangement of fresh flowers.

Now she'd get some value from it—entertainment—watching whoever picked it up, whether they kept mum or crowed.

Her phone beeped. Her heart danced. But the text was only from Quentrell.

Got the tens in the jar?

Oh, right. She pulled three ten-dollar bills from her own wallet and put them in the tip jar. Quentrell's trick to shame generosity from the next cycle of tippers.

Maddie earned $100 to $300 a night checking coats, but it was seasonal work. Warmer weather marooned her to the hostess station. More visibility, less money.

She texted back: *Thx for reminder.*

Then, so she wouldn't text Lester again, at least not until he responded to her six earlier texts, she began rolling on her stool up and down the narrow aisle between the two racks of coats. Her nose filled with the smells of the coat owners: a nose-itching blend of perfume, cigarettes, booze, marijuana, and tonight, someone's body odor. At least tonight nothing smelled of moth balls, but management still hadn't replaced the overhead fluorescent tube which flickered in headache-inducing spasms.

"Damn," she muttered. She felt a headache coming on, but she knew she couldn't blame the coat smells or flickering fluorescent.

"I'm losing you, aren't I," she whispered. She clenched her fists and kept rolling. Lester's visits had shrunk to once a week, and not on the best night, but on a Monday or Tuesday evening. He wasn't staying over anymore. He wasn't complaining about his wife anymore. He hadn't brought Maddie flowers or wine or Chinese takeout in weeks.

Most dire of all, he wasn't returning her texts.

She grabbed her phone and texted Quentrell:

So many animals have given their skins to swaddle the diners who r now chomping the flesh of other wretched animals. My coat check room is a mausoleum. U can use this in one of your poems if u want.

He texted right back.

That make u the crypt keeper?

Maddie texted a smile back.

Was that what she was? A crypt keeper?
A hypocrite for sure.

***

They'd met ten months ago at a Lexus dealership.

Lester had walked in alone, late morning, the first customer of the day. He stopped and looked at her name plaque on the receptionist desk.

"Good morning, Maddie Silk," he said. "You are as lovely as your name."

She rolled her eyes, used to the male customers' flirtatious behavior. She never let it go anywhere. Most of them didn't intend it to go anywhere anyway.

"I am here," he said, "to buy a Lexus for my wife's 40th birthday."

"What makes you think you'll find anything here?" was her inane response, but he laughed anyway. A laugh that crinkled his eyes and dimpled his right cheek.

He was in the manager's office, signing papers for a Lexus, when she left for lunch.

She was sitting in a window booth, waiting for salad and spaghetti, and reading the current issue of *The Week*, when a shadow darkened her table.

She looked up. Lester stood outside the window, waving and smiling.

She nodded and the next thing she knew he was standing at her booth, his silver hair salted with streaks of midnight, his eyes blue as Lake Michigan on a sunny day, and his scent fresh and woodsy, reminding her of the newly framed homes she'd help build one summer for Habitat for Humanity.

"Hey, Mr. Lexus Shopper," she said. "So you bought a car?"

"It's Lester," he replied. "Lester Larkin. I did, and may I join you?"

She must have assented, for he slid across from her and opened a menu.

"What do you recommend, Maddie Silk?"

"I always get the iceberg wedge and spaghetti."

"Hmm," he said. "I've just spent too much money on a silver Lexus, and I think I need a hefty dose of animal protein. So?"

She shook her head. "I'm a vegetarian. Have been since my freshman year in college."

He set the menu down.

"You're going to want me to leave then."

Bubbles were popping in her stomach, and her heart was beating very fast.

"And why's that?"

"Before I tell you, you have to tell me. What happened your freshman year in college that put you in the enemy camp?"

"Enemy camp? What are you, a butcher?"

He laughed. "You first. Tell me why."

"If you'd taken the Animal Ethics class I had my freshman year, you'd be vegetarian too. I lost my taste for meat after I saw how animals on factory farms suffer to satisfy human appetites."

"So." He looked at the menu. "I take it the chicken parmesan is off limits?"

"Living chickens have their beaks sliced off so they can't peck each other in their tightly packed cages."

He nodded. "That is bad." He studied the menu. "Pork chops?"

"Pigs—they're smarter than dogs, by the way—spend their shortened lives in windowless sheds without fresh air, sunlight, or outdoor access. They live in their own waste, and the high ammonia levels from their waste burn their eyes, throats, and skin."

He shook his head. "That's even worse. So I'm not even going to ask about the hamburger."

"I don't blame you. No one wants to hear how cows are castrated to improve the taste of meat, dehorned to reduce injury when they fight, have their tails amputated to reduce the spread of disease. All without anesthetics. And baby cows? Their tongues are amputated to prevent sucking problems."

He sighed. Closed the menu. "I take it you got an A in that class."

"I got A's in all my classes as it happens. How do you think I landed the job as a receptionist at the Lexus dealership?"

He laughed. The waitress approached. "I'll have what she's having," he said.

Maddie felt like she'd melt into the plastic seat cushion. "Thank you." Her voice broke.

He reached across the table, placed his hand over hers. His wedding ring, a simple gold band, shot sunlight into her eyes. "I hereby promise you, Maddie Silk, to never ever again eat animal in your presence, but only if you'll forgive me."

"For what?" *What was he implying? That he wanted a future with her? They'd just met! He was married! He was gorgeous! He was probably rich!*

"For owning, along with my partners, some restaurants that serve lots of meat. Our little flagship you may have heard of. *That Steak Place.*"

To her horror, she heard herself laugh. Of course she knew *That Steak Place.* Everyone did. Reservations had to be made months in advance. Celebrities, sports heroes, and political hotshots dined there.

"I like it when you laugh," he said, "even if it's at me."

She stopped laughing. "I'm not laughing at you. I'm laughing at me."

"Sorry?"

"You're like the anti-me. You're rich, old, married. And a carnivore."

"Old?"

She could see she'd actually insulted him. His cheeks flamed red.

"Sorry. Not old old. I mean you're what, forty? Fifty?"

He frowned. "Forty-four. And you are?"

"Young enough to be your daughter."

He looked out the window. Sighed. When he looked back at her, she was shocked to see tears welling in his eyes.

"Hey." She reached across the table, touched his clenched fists. "I'm sorry. You're being nice. And I'm being rude."

He shook his head. "No. No, you're not being rude. It's just that, you found my Achilles heel. I'm not going to ever have a daughter. Or a son. I had leukemia when I was a kid. And the cure, well, the cure killed that possibility."

For a long moment, they just looked at each other.

Their lunch stretched into the dinner hour. She found herself telling him things she'd never told anyone before. She'd never been listened to the way Lester listened to her. She told Lester how she'd always figured she'd become a lawyer like her dad, who'd died of a heart attack her freshman year in high school, leaving her alone with an indifferent mother. She told Lester how her early academic sparkle (she'd been double promoted twice in grade school) had dissipated in high school into a frenzy of cliques, hookups, and partying. She told Lester how law school had never happened. She'd scored too low on the LSATs (due to a perfect storm of hangover, headache, and heartache) to get any scholarship money, and by the time she graduated at age 19 from NIU, she was tired of books and out of money.

Now, she told Lester, she was twenty years old, barely getting by with a mind-numbing job as a receptionist at the Lexus dealership, and living with roaches in a dark studio on Wilson Avenue in the iffy Uptown neighborhood.

***

Two weeks later, she was making $100 to $300 a night as a coat check girl at *That Steak Place* and paying crazy low rent for a sunny, modern one bedroom in a high rise with a view of Lake Michigan. The apartment was owned by Lester's good friend who was more interested, Lester assured her, in having a good tenant like Maddie than in gouging a bad tenant with market rate rent.

Glynn, Lester's wife, loved the Lexus he bought for her 40th birthday. Lester loved it, too.

"It's the Lexus," he said to Maddie, "that brought you into my life."

Maddie googled Glynn Larkin and found photos of a big-boned, sturdy, woman with a jaw like Jay Leno's and large square teeth.

Glynn looked a little like Eleanor Roosevelt, Maddie thought, but with better hair.

Glynn, Maddie learned, had inherited lots of money. She'd been the only child of a Sony movie producer and a U.S. Senator's daughter.

Glynn, Maddie learned from Lester, did not want children.

"It's my one big heartbreak," Lester said to Maddie over their first Chinese takeout in her new apartment overlooking Lake Michigan. "We'd talked about alternative ways to become parents, Glynn and me. Adoption, of course. But other ways too. But Glynn kept putting it off, and now she says she's too old, too impatient, to be a mother."

Suddenly, he blushed. He stared down at his bowl of meatless fried rice. "I'm sorry," he murmured. "I shouldn't be dumping this on you."

Maddie felt her heart tremble. She stood. Took his hand. Led him to her bed.

Afterwards, spooned together under her down-filled comforter, he whispered into her ear. "Thank you, Maddie Silk. I knew you'd understand."

"You will be a father someday, Lester," she said. She pressed his palm over her heart. "A great father."

And maybe someday, she thought, *we'll be parents together.*

***

Maddie stopped mid-roll in the middle of the coats in the coat check room.

"Oh my God," she said.

The poker chip! It was from Lester! It had to be! He'd had someone drop it in her tip jar, knowing she would show it to him the next time (hopefully tonight) they were together. She'd be complaining about the bozo who'd put it in her tip jar, and he'd say something goofy-sweet like "don't call me a bozo, Mad-girl," and she'd say, "what are you talking about?" and then it would hit her, and she'd fling her arms around him as he said, "pack your bags, we're going to Vegas, happy birthday Maddie, sorry it's late, but business blah blah blah."

Maddie shot from her stool and ran to the counter. She was about to dash out and grab the chip off the floor when a blast of cold air alerted her to incoming diners.

Maddie stayed put, readied her smile, and awaited the two couples approaching her.

A leather jacket covered a man. He was bald, pudgy, short.

A leather biker jacket covered his companion. She was young, curvy, curly-haired, tall. They held hands and were twisting their heads to talk to the couple behind them.

The second couple came into Maddie's view. Her heart sputtered. Her mouth went dry.

Lester.

Lester, holding hands with a blonde beauty.

Lester was wearing his Versace Navy Wool Double Breasted Pea coat. Maddie had been with him when he'd bought it.

The gorgeous blonde wore a blackplum-colored Burberry London Cashmere Trench Coat whose two vertical rows of large gold dome buttons (for a military vibe) were perfectly aligned.

The flawless twin of Maddie's flawed coat.

"Welcome to *That Steak Place*," Maddie said. She kept her voice pleasant and her eyes on the bald man's coat.

"Thank you, sweetheart." The bald man placed his jacket on the counter.

Despite the shock waves roiling through her body, she couldn't stop her practiced eye from identifying the jacket. *Cole Haan Espresso Lambskin Leather Jacket, $700.*

The bald man's curvy companion slipped off her biker jacket and held it out to the man.

"This thing weighs a ton," she said as he took the jacket from her.

"That's why I'm not a leather fan," the blonde beauty said.

Lester placed his own coat on the counter. He turned to the blonde beauty.

"Lola?" he murmured. He helped Lola slip out of her coat. Maddie stared at Lola's tanned, toned, bare arms. *You'll be chilly,* she thought.

"Four coats to check?" Maddie asked. Her heart pounded, but her voice, she thought, sounded calm.

The bald man laughed. "We got an Einstein here, Les." He poked a fat finger into the four coats on the counter. *"Un, deux, trois, quatre,"* he said. "That's one-two-three-four in Swahili."

Everyone laughed but Lester and Maddie. Maddie smiled though it hurt her face. Lester smiled, but at Lola, not Maddie.

Maddie pulled four tickets from the bowl on the counter. She split them and placed one stub atop each coat.

She handed the other four stubs to Lester. He leaned close.

"Thank you," he said in a low voice. "I knew you'd understand."

She watched them move toward the hostess station.

Her heart pounding, she called out, "Enjoy your dinner. Fulks."

Only Lester turned his head toward her. He smiled, shot her a thumbs up.

"Oh my God!" Lola cried. "Look!" She plucked the chip from the floor. "Lester! Can you believe it! A five-dollar chip from the Venetian! Now we'll have to stay there next week! It's a sign!"

Maddie gripped the counter so she wouldn't collapse. Lola had taken everything. Her chip. Her Vegas trip. Her Lester.

She watched the hostess lead them into the restaurant. Lester, an owner, didn't need to wait for the next scheduled seating. A prime window table was always reserved for the owners.

She hung their coats. She sat on her stool. She texted Quentrell.

U realize that was Lester u just let in. With his new girlfriend Lola. Guess that's how he's breaking up w/me. This is the man I dreamed I'd marry.

Right away, Quentrell texted back.

Yup. He such a cool dude he fist bump me and say howya be Quinn. Been working for the dude five years he still don't get my name right. Anyway, girl, good riddance to that rich old guy contaminating your life. The only rich old guy a good girl like u should marry is rich old guy who at least ninety. Come celebrate yr liberation w/me & Mark after work?

Good girl? Was she a good girl? Quentrell was a good guy. And *he* thought she was a good girl.

Despite her sick heart, Maddie smiled, thinking how rejuvenated she always felt after spending time with Mark and Quentrell. They were probably the most stable, loving couple she knew. Mark reminded her of her own father, dead eight years now. He had a booming laugh, like her father, and could fix anything, like her father.

She texted *maybe* back to Quentrell.

She waited for her breathing to settle, for her heart to stop palpitating. Then she rolled on her stool to where she'd hung Lola's coat.

She pulled Lola's coat into her lap and inspected it. Her hands shook as she ran them over the coat. Same size as her own coat, but perfect. No stains. No rips. Her mouth felt dry. Her legs wobbled as she stood and carried the coat to the counter. Her eyes burned as she crouched before the bin on the floor holding her things.

She closed her eyes for a long moment. She opened them. She swapped coats.

The perfect coat belonging to Lola went into Maddie's storage bin.

Maddie's flawed twin coat went on the hanger.

Wait.

Maddie unbuttoned the front pockets on the perfect coat. She found a pack of Virginia Slim menthols, Visine eye drops, a glass pipe that smelled of marijuana, and a business card for a place called High Jinques whose e-mail address included 420, slang for dope.

She transferred the items to the same front pockets on her coat, now destined to shroud the young (probably drug-addled) bones of the beautiful Lola.

She returned to the coat check counter just as a thin brown woman trudged by.

"Hey, Venita," Maddie said. "Going home early?" Venita Trapp was one of the kitchen staff who mostly sliced, diced, and scrubbed.

A hair net still webbed Venita's braided black hair.

"Jus' got a call from the sitter. She sick, stuff coming out both ends. Gotta get home to my boy so the sitter can get home to her *own* toilet."

Maddie laughed. The laugh felt good. The laugh broke the thickness that had been clogging Maddie's throat.

Maddie looked at the thin blue windbreaker Venita was wearing and shook her head. "Where's your coat, Venita? It's bad out there!"

Venita unzipped the windbreaker, revealing the knitted sweater underneath. "Jus' two blocks to the El from here. My apartment building's jus' a block from where I get off."

Maddie sighed. She reached down to her bin on the floor, grabbed Lola's coat, placed it on the counter.

"Hey. Take this one, Venita. Stay warm."

"What you gonna wear home then, Maddie?" Venita's eyes glistened as she reached for the coat.

Maddie shrugged. "There are usually one or two coats abandoned by the end of the night. Who knows why. I can borrow one of those. I'll be fine. Go on. Put it on. Let's see how it fits."

It was just a little big on Venita, but the dark purple color suited her.

"Mmm, smell good too, Maddie. What your perfume, girl? Smell like that Juicy Couture. I test sprayed it at Ulta jus' the other day. That serious money, Maddie!"

"Birthday gift, Venita," Maddie lied. "Juicy Couture perfume from my mom."

What her recently remarried mother had actually sent to Maddie from her condo in Naples, Florida, was a card containing twenty-one crisp dollar bills, a dollar for each year of Maddie's life.

Twenty-one dollars didn't buy much. She'd spent it in a bar with her girlfriend. Two glasses of chardonnay plus tip.

Was that why she'd let wealthy Lester into her life?

What did that make her? Venita was talking, but her voice seemed far away, background music to the feelings suddenly roaring through Maddie's body.

Her anger at Lola, Lester's new love, evaporated. Maddie had no standing to be outraged at Lola. She and Lola were both trespassers, both of them trespassing on another woman's marriage. Funny in an ironic sort of way, Maddie thought, how it took being trespassed against to recognize her own transgression. Not that she hadn't known Lester was married. But she hadn't *felt* the harm. Until now.

The harm felt sharp and venomous, a poison arrow piercing her self-esteem.

"I'll return your coat next shift, Maddie," Venita said as she headed for the door.

"No hurry," Maddie called out. "The color looks better on you than me anyway."

Maddie checked the time on her phone. Soon the current cycle of diners would be finishing up, coming for their coats. They'd be followed by incoming diners for the next scheduled seating. Maddie had maybe ten minutes of solitude left.

It was now or never.

She took back the three ten-dollar bills she'd planted in her tip jar. She gathered her things from the bin, put on her boots, then slowly marched the narrow aisle between the coats, running her hands along the leathers, cashmeres, furs, wools.

She stopped by Lester's coat. She put it on. Too big, of course. She knew what he'd paid for it. $1,295.

She smiled. Sell it on Craigslist. That would cover two months' rent. And leave something for a small donation to the American Society for the Prevention of Cruelty to Animals. *ASPCA* was her favorite charity, but it had been too long since she'd sent any money to them. So maybe she should just leave her sunny apartment with a view of Lake Michigan—she hadn't signed a lease, of course—and go back to the roaches. Yep. She'd do that, and then she could give a bigger donation to the ASPCA.

She checked the pockets on Lester's coat. Nothing but a ball point pen. Perfect. She used it to write a note on the ticket stub on the new empty hanger.

Thanks, Les. I know you'll understand.

She rummaged in her tote, found her apartment key. She put the key in the front pocket of Lester's coat—now hers.

She strode to the thick glass door. Quentrell opened it. Raised his eyebrows at the coat she was wearing.

"Was Les behind the wheel?" she asked Quentrell. She put her right hand in the coat pocket, gripped the key.

She'd never keyed a car in her life.

"If it's Lester's car," she said, "I've got a message to leave on it for him." She removed the key from her pocket and held it up.

Quentrell looked at the key. Then he looked at her a long moment, pursed his lips. He sighed. Nodded. "Red Benz. You wanna know where it at?"

"Would you tell me, Quentrell?"

"Maddie, you my friend. My *good* friend. So. If you want me to . . ."

She returned the key to the coat pocket.

"No." She shook her head. "There's some lines I won't cross. But you know, I like having the choice."

She held out her hand. Quentrell gripped it, shook it. "Thank you, Quentrell. My good friend. For being willing to cross for me."

He nodded. Gave her a salute. "You a good girl, Maddie."

She hugged him, promised to see him and Mark later. Then she left *That Steak Place*.

For good.

Laurie Whitman
Not Just Another Coat

In 1994, my kids and I won a prize. Not just a prize, but a **PRIZE.** I say my kids and I won, but my son will correct me by saying that it was **his** *Sports Illustrated for Kids* subscription that helped us win the prize—but I'm the one who paid for the subscription, and I'm the one who sent in the renewal form.

At the time, I had no idea I was entering a contest. I had subscribed to the magazine since its inception when my son was 8 years old, so this was my fourth renewal. I received a letter via FedEx stating that I was a potential winner in the *SI for Kids* sweepstakes.

Oh, great, I probably won a football lamp. I ignored the letter.

A week later, I received a telephone call from the accounting firm that was overseeing the sweepstakes. The woman who called advised me to return the form; it was a dated prize and I had to send it in as soon as possible. She could not reveal the prize until my paperwork was completed.

Wow. It was January. I was thinking . . . Super Bowl!

I signed the affidavit, had it notarized, and sent it via Fed Ex to the correct party.

The next day, saying good-bye to my kids as they left for school, I told them that when they got home, we may know what we won. By this time, we all were curious and excited.

I waited anxiously for the phone call. At three minutes after two, the call came. The caller was a woman. She began to talk in a fast, raspy voice. I listened, dumbstruck.

"Your prize," she told me, "is for one child and two adults to spend five days in Lillehammer, Norway, for the 1994 Olympic Games! Travel expenses included!"

My heart sank. "I'm a single mom with two kids . . . could we all go?"

She said she'd find out.

Twenty minutes later, she called me back.

"Yes!"

We flew to New York, then on to Oslo, and took a long bus ride to Lillehammer. We were the guests of honor, and my kids were the only kids on the trip. My son was 12; my daughter was 8.

Upon arrival at the Quality Inn, we each received a package of goodies—a hat, a scarf, butt warmers, hand warmers, cow bells, lovely authentic Norwegian sweaters with the pictograms knitted into the design, and a gorgeous Columbia 4-in-1 jacket. Each item proudly displayed the *Sports Illustrated* logo designed especially for the Olympics. The *SI colors* were royal blue and black. We had badges, too, that allowed us into the sponsor tent. Food and drink were available all day.

It was a whirlwind five days. My kids got to give the flowers to the American ice dancers; we observed skiing; we saw Bonnie Blair get her fifth medal. We went on an authentic dog sled ride and ended up for lunch at a quaint inn hidden away in the woods. We ate lots of elk, had lingonberries on our ice cream, and we all tried herring! We attended a special banquet where some of the 1980 ice hockey team were in attendance, along with Jean Claude Killy and Kristi Yamaguchi.

And snow! They do not use salt in Norway, but rather sand on the roads and walkways. So, the whole place remained sparkling white. It was cold but so sunny and beautiful.

Everyone wears those heavy sweaters indoors and out because heat is scanty.

One night our entire group of 100+ people ventured to a restaurant. The restaurant was small and reserved for our group that evening. The rounded thatch-type roof was mounded with layers and layers of snow, each layer indicating a new snowfall. The snow on the roof was at least three feet high.

When we walked in, the first thing I noticed was the coat rack—hundreds of the exact same coat. I worried. How would I find my coat? And my kids' coats? Our three "prize" coats were exact matches to all of those hanging on the rack—a sea of royal blue and black.

I checked my coat pockets: tissue, coins, lip gloss. Maybe I should transfer that stuff to my purse?

Then I spotted the coat check girl. Ruddy cheeked, laughing, welcoming us into the establishment, joyfully taking the identical coats and handing each of us our coat tag: our insurance that we would get the right coat.

I left my stuff in my coat pockets.

Twenty-one years later, I still wear my royal blue and black prize coat. I actually have three of them hanging in my closet. (Kids don't want to wear the same thing as the mom!) So I can wear any combination of the available pieces—from a double jacket suited for below zero temperatures to a day at the beginning of spring.

Margo Rife
Hang in There, Hamlet

"In 1965, director Peter Hall cast 24-year-old David Warner to play his *Hamlet*. Hall wanted to attract a youthful audience to the production and did so by presenting Hamlet as a contemporary youth, disillusioned by the world around him. The look of Hamlet was quite significant. He was scruffy in his appearance and attire, wearing a moth-eaten black gown and red scarf, looking every inch a university undergraduate." *BBC Hamlet Past Productions*

The play was a great success. *Hang in There, Hamlet* is based on this moment in history.

This play is dedicated to everyone who, at one point or another, failed to take a risk. "To risk or not to risk...that is the question."

CHARACTERS

CARL: Middle-aged director of professional theater group.
JEFF: Struggling actor in his twenties with ADHD tendencies dressed in a thrift store long black frayed coat and long thin red scarf.
HORATIO: Loyal actor friend of Jeff's. Actual name is Horatio. He is dressed in an elaborate Elizabethan style coat.
JEFF'S FATHER/GHOST: Middle-aged man in Elizabethan coat and crown.

SETTING: A small theater space in a metro area in America, 1965.

AT RISE: Theater with appropriate props for staging of Hamlet. Director seated stage right.

JEFF: *(Races down the aisle of theater.)* "Oh that this too too solid flesh would melt."

CARL: You know what's melting? My patience. You're late again. Very unprofessional.

JEFF: So sorry, Carl. My dog threw up on my coat.

CARL: That's the best you can come up with? It's just a variation on the dog ate my homework.

JEFF: He ate a whole pound of salami. Even the skin.

CARL: I don't want to hear that. And don't call me Carl.

JEFF: Sorry, Carl. What do I call you?

CARL: Mr. Klaus. I deserve a mister moniker, don't you think? I've been in theater for over thirty years. What's it been for you? A year?

JEFF: Two and a half years, 300 hours, 36 minutes.

CARL: Enough. Let's move on. You do remember the importance of today?

JEFF: Yes, sir. First full dress rehearsal. All hands on deck.

CARL: Please no nautical clichés. They make me seasick.

JEFF: Sorry, sir. But no need to worry. I've been up all night researching my soliloquy.

CARL: Not again! Always living in your books. You're not going to find greatness in a library. Your mind floats up there in the proscenium. But you need your feet planted on the ground. See this wood floor? It's stained with sweat, makeup and tears. This is where you draw your inspiration. Are you listening to me?

JEFF: *(frantically searching coat pocket.)* Sorry, Carl. Mr. Klaus. I think I left my notes at home.

CARL: Losing things? Arriving late? Distracted? What the hell is wrong with you?

JEFF: I'm hyperactive, Mr. Klaus.

CARL: Hyperactive? You're an adult not a child. Now go get yourself suited up for rehearsal so we can go over the soliloquy. I don't want to hear one more excuse.

JEFF: Sir, this play is my life. I eat, sleep and drink Shakespeare.

CARL: Go. Get out of here. We start in five.

(Carl exits. Jeff hurries to a folding screen/wardrobe stage left and searches for his Hamlet coat. Horatio enters.)

HORATIO: Hey, bro. How do I look? *(Horatio turns so that Jeff can see his Elizabethan costume.)*

JEFF: You look classy, dude.

HORATIO: I know. Can you take a photo of me?

JEFF: Can't. Don't see my velvet coat. I know I put it here last week.

HORATIO: You lent it to Jamie.

JEFF: What?

HORATIO: Yeah. We were at Lisa's party. You were a little stoned. Well, a lot.

JEFF: That was some wicked weed.

HORATIO: Well, Jamie said he was going to meet his new lady love and wanted to borrow your velvet Hamlet coat. You told him, "Go ahead."

JEFF: But I wasn't wearing the coat at Lisa's. It's always with wardrobe.

HORATIO: Jamie knows that. When he wants something, he always knows where to find it.

JEFF: So where's my freaking coat, Horatio?

HORATIO: Ask Jamie.

JEFF: I can't, dude. I'm expected onstage in five minutes.

HORATIO: Don't panic. We'll find it. He probably put it back.

JEFF: I roomed with the guy for two years. He never put anything back.

HORATIO: Why don't I run to the corner and call him on the pay phone? You keep looking. And hey, remember as Shakespeare said, "neither a borrower nor a lender be."

JEFF: Yeah. Yeah. "For loan oft loses both itself and friend."

HORATIO: Hang in there, Hamlet. I'm here for you.

JEFF: Hurry! *(Jeff talks to himself as he looks for lost coat.)* Holy crap. I am in such big trouble. Calm down. Deep breath. It's not that bad. It's not like my uncle killed my father and married my mother. No. It's just a lost coat.

(Low moaning sound)

JEFF: Who's there?

(Louder moaning sound)

JEFF: Horatio? Is that you? Not funny.

(silence)

JEFF: Come out, or I'm going to knock down this screen. One, two...

(Ghost dressed in kingly attire walks around screen into view and addresses Jeff in Shakespearean manner.)

GHOST: Mark me.

JEFF: What the...?

GHOST: Jeff. It's your father.

JEFF: Dad?

GHOST: Mark my words, son.

JEFF: But you're dead, Dad.

GHOST: I have come back from the underworld.

JEFF: Why are you here? In this theater?

GHOST: To be the voice of reason.

JEFF: What? But that's all you've ever been. The voice of reason.

GHOST: Mark my words.

JEFF: Why are you talking like the King of Denmark? It's creepy.

GHOST: Because you never listened to your "old man" as you referred to me.

JEFF: I never paid attention because all you did was lecture.

GHOST: Mark me, son. My time is short.

JEFF: Not as short as mine. I've got four minutes, Dad. Can you please get on with it?

GHOST: I'm here to warn you to abandon this lunatic dream of being an actor.

JEFF: You're kidding, right? You braved the underworld to present that same old pitch?

GHOST: What father can rest knowing that his son is going into the Arts?

JEFF: Dad.

GHOST: Since time immortal, it is the duty of fathers to block their sons from going into the Arts. Music. Painting. Dance. But most of all, theater.

JEFF: I'm not cut out for business, Dad. You know that. Remember that summer I interned at your company? The work crews would corral me and shoot me with rubber bands. They knew I didn't belong in that world.

GHOST: Before I died, I talked to the night manager at the deli. He agreed to extend your hours to full time. It's a start, son. People will always want pastrami.

JEFF: Oh my God! You wasted a trip, Dad. In three minutes my boss is going to kick me off the stage and out to the street. It's back to the deli slicer. I'll be smelling like salami the rest of my life. Happy?

GHOST: Why so angry, son? I tried to help you all through childhood but you were always so distracted. Unable to sit still. Broke every toy. Handed in every assignment late.

JEFF: Dad, we've been through this a thousand times. I'm on a deadline now, and if I fail, it will affect the rest of my life!

GHOST: I will leave now, son. But you have doomed me to walk the earth. I have failed as a father.

JEFF: I'm sorry you feel that way. But your life is over. Mine is just beginning. I need to find that coat. It's life or death for me. Understand?

(Ghost roars. Jeff cowers. Ghost exits.)

JEFF: *(Turns and faces audience.)* Okay. Okay. What would Hamlet do? First, he wouldn't ask anyone for help. Hamlet thinks well on his feet. Second, Hamlet likes to think outside the box. Third, "The play's the thing."

CARL: *(Offstage calls out to crew.)* Crew, get ready for first full dress. Lighting, sound, everything. Jeff? Are you ready? Who are you talking to?

JEFF: Yes, Mr. Klaus. One minute. Practicing my lines.

CARL: Take care of that velvet coat. Rosa worked overtime taking it in and adding ruffles.

JEFF: I remember, sir. I thanked her.

CARL: *(Offstage addresses workers.)* Get that working spotlight ready, Joe. Let's go with that angle we discussed. Set design. Nice job. You captured the castle. Everyone else. Remember your marks.

(Horatio comes running in.)

JEFF: Where's the coat?

HORATIO: You won't believe this! Jamie left it at a bar. He went back to check, but someone had made off with it. It's gone, Jeff.

JEFF: *(Groans.)* No! I can't play Hamlet in this coat.

HORATIO: It's looking bad for you. But I'll back you up.

JEFF: No way. You've got a career going, man. Your grandma was right in naming you Horatio. You rule that part.

HORATIO: Thanks.

JEFF: Besides, no one goes against Carl Klaus and wins.

HORATIO: You got that right.

CARL: Hamlet! On stage now or I'll call your understudy.

JEFF: Horatio? What do I do?

HORATIO: Face the music, man.

JEFF: Can I borrow your coat?

HORATIO: No way. This play is my ticket to a better place. Off Off Broadway.

JEFF: What about "I'm here for you, dude?"

HORATIO: Look. Carl will know it's my coat. It won't fit you anyway.

JEFF: You owe me one. Big time.

(Horatio exits stage left.)

CARL: *(Offstage.)* What's going on back there?

(Jeff hides behind screen. Carl enters stage right.)

CARL: Are we adults or children who need supervision?

JEFF: I... I....

CARL: Aye, aye? I warned you about nautical phrases.

(Jeff steps out from behind folding screen.)

CARL: What is this? Where's the coat? Don't you know what a dress rehearsal is? A dress rehearsal means you need to be in costume.

JEFF: Right.

CARL: *(Jabs his finger into Jeff's coat.) That* is not your velvet coat. *That* is your street wear. Your thrift-store coat that you're so thrilled about.

JEFF: I do love this coat, sir. It's me.

CARL: *(Repeatedly jabs Jeff in chest.)* We don't want *you.* We want Hamlet. Prince of Denmark. In his velvet coat. With ruffles.

JEFF: But Mr. Klaus, why does Hamlet have to be a period piece?

CARL: Hamlet was written as an Elizabethan Age play whose characters dress in Elizabethan attire.

JEFF: But this is 1965. Why so formal?

CARL: You're distracting me again. Where's the coat?

JEFF: Please, Mr. Klaus. Just hear me out.

CARL: I'm on a tight schedule.

JEFF: Well, what if we did something a little different?

CARL: Like replace you with your understudy?

JEFF: Why do we have to stage the traditional formal Elizabethan Hamlet with four hours of the melancholy Dane in a gloomy setting?

CARL: You are not wearing that hippie thrift store coat!

JEFF: Sir, I step out on the stage in this coat and scarf and it will be like opening a window in the catacombs. It will stir the dust. Breathe new life. Energize.

CARL: Shakespeare never gets old. Hamlet is timeless.

JEFF: Shakespeare's *themes* never get old.

CARL: Revenge is something everyone relates to.

JEFF: We can agree on that. Hamlet is about a son, a father, a mother, a girlfriend and uncle.

CARL: Set among royalty in a castle in Denmark.

JEFF: But you took the first step in brushing off the dust.

CARL: How's that?

JEFF: Hamlet's uncle Claudius is the villain, but you didn't dress him all in black, did you?

CARL: Of course not.

JEFF: You don't have him giving the audience furtive glances. You play him like a cold, calculating murderer. It's modern.

CARL: So glad to get your approval. That's sarcasm by the way. I do like subtleties. Your hippie outfit is not subtle.

JEFF: It's not blasphemy either for audiences to not be sure of the decade.

CARL: It will confuse our audience.

JEFF: It will only confuse the theatergoers who remember Laurence Olivier.

CARL: The older audience is our mainstay. Middle age. Middle class.

JEFF: But how about attracting young people? A wronged youth who's misunderstood is the perfect plot.

CARL: I must admit it would be refreshing to play to an audience who doesn't know the outcome.

JEFF: Who've never even seen a Shakespearean play!

CARL: That's a frightening thought.

JEFF: You could be known as the director who speaks to the youth of this country!

(Horatio enters)

HORATIO: Sorry for interrupting, Mr. Klaus, but Jeff is spot on.

CARL: You too, Horatio?

HORATIO: Unlike Jeff, I don't think you will fire me for speaking out.

CARL: Why is that?

HORATIO: Because I'm the best Horatio you'll ever find. I was born for this.

CARL: True. Go on.

HORATIO: Haven't you noticed that your niece and her friends hang around here after school?

CARL: Yes. But I don't see. . .

HORATIO: They're not here to see you, Mr. Klaus. Or me. They want the scruffy, slouchy Hamlet who sometimes mumbles.

CARL: My niece and her little friends will not be writing my theatrical review.

HORATIO: But the critics will catch their youthful excitement.

CARL: A scruffy, mumbling Hamlet with a moth-eaten coat. I can hear the laughter.

JEFF: With my "hippie thrift store" coat, Mr. Klaus, you could be known as the director who challenges the audience. Isn't it worth that risk?

CARL: Do you think I don't know about taking risks?

JEFF: You seem risk adverse.

CARL: Tell me. Why do directors fear risk?

JEFF: Fear of failure?

CARL: Exactly.

JEFF: Maybe you need to fail in a grander way.

CARL: Oh, but I already excel at failure.

(Loud voice offstage yells "GERTRUDE!" in a Brando-like voice.)

CARL: *(Visibly cringing.)* Failure and I are old friends.

(Loud Brando-like voice offstage: "GERTRUDE!")

CARL: I'm going to come backstage, Joe!

JEFF: Who's Gertrude?

CARL: My first failure.

HORATIO: Oh yeah. I remember hearing about that. *Streetcar Named Desire.* Instead of Stella . . .

CARL: Gertrude.

JEFF: Why the name change?

CARL: If you must know, I promised my dying grandmother that the next play I directed would have a character named—

JEFF: Gertrude? Holy cow, Carl.

CARL: I told you! Don't call me Carl. It's Mr. Klaus. Now take off that ridiculous coat. We're staging Hamlet with lavish scenic design, impeccable performances, and flawless lighting. Your coat is not invited.

JEFF: You know what my friends call that?

HORATIO: Museum Theater.

CARL: Do they now?

HORATIO: A classic can't escape its contemporary context.

JEFF: Look out on the street. It's a new age. The Beatles, mini-skirts. It's not the wrong coat, it's the right moment.

CARL: So you picture Polonius in suede fringe and Hamlet's mother in white go-go boots?

JEFF: No, not all the cast. But I think there are other actors who can throw off the Elizabethan garb.

CARL: Horatio?

HORATIO: Please, please?

JEFF: Rosencrantz and Guildenstern too. I like that you've made them funny.

CARL: Maybe Ophelia as a flower child. She seems like a young woman from Iowa who suddenly finds herself on the Sunset Strip among the loonies.

JEFF: That's what I thought.

CARL: Any other brilliant ideas?

JEFF: Are you being sarcastic?

CARL: No.

JEFF: Do I have to sound so formal in my soliloquy? Can't we try for a more conversational tone?

CARL: You're pushing it, Jeff.

JEFF: Can we give it a try, Carl?

CARL: Horatio. Act II Scene 5.

(Horatio smiles and gives Jeff a thumbs up. Then he rips off his Elizabethan coat and flings it to the floor.)

Barry Abrams
Redemption

"Good morning Melissa."

I came out of my reverie as Dr. Benson, a cheerful, friendly man, entered the room.

"So I hear that you've been having problems with your asthma this week."

"This is the third time in the past five weeks."

"That must be very frustrating. Let's see what we can do to fix the problem."

He studied my chart which gave me time to admire his closely cropped salt and pepper hair, his well-groomed goatee, and his wedding band. He was elegant and looked much younger than his sixty years. Even though he was too old for me, I bemoaned that the cute, employed ones were always taken.

He examined me, and I felt better after an albuterol treatment and steroid injection. Afterwards, we worked together on my Asthma Plan.

We discussed my triggers and the need to stay away from my friends when they are smoking. He also let me have it about not taking my allergy meds and drinking too much coffee and alcohol on weekends. Both trigger my reflux, and therefore my asthma.

I make my living as an athlete, and I was worried that my performance would be affected. I had been quite winded at workouts for the past week, and because I teach Tae Kwon Do, kick boxing, and work as a personal trainer, I have to be at my best.

I thanked Dr. Benson and shoved all worries aside. I grabbed my coat off the rack in the waiting room, waved to the receptionist, and headed to the gym for a steam and shower.

An hour later, I was at my front door, but as I fumbled for my keys, I found something in the pocket that wasn't mine. I pulled out a small wallet containing money, credit cards, and a driver's license. Damn it! I had the wrong coat!

A girl smiled at me through a see-through pocket. She looked like she was twelve, one of those people who would likely be carded for the rest of her life. I examined the contents of her wallet, found her number, and called her right away.

"Hello?"

"Is this Samantha Weiss?"

Silence. I tried again. "Samantha? Samantha Weiss?"

A sigh. Then a whispered, "Yes, this is she."

"Hi, my name's Melissa Williston, and I have your wallet and coat. I have the same coat and must have grabbed yours by mistake at the doctor's office. I'd like to meet with you to switch. I'm sorry for the inconvenience."

"Maybe I should be the one apologizing? I was in a rush to leave Dr. Benson's, and I grabbed your coat by mistake. Thank you so much for calling. You didn't have any ID in your pockets. I have your keys, and I'm sure you need them. I can meet you at a restaurant called *Jesse's Place*? How about one hour?"

"Great! It's my favorite. I'll see you then."

***

Jesse's Place is a refurbished old speakeasy with mood lighting and high-backed solid oak seating polished to glass smoothness from ninety years of patrons sliding their bodies into each booth. The entrance has an inviting, well-lit atmosphere which becomes more subdued toward the back, if privacy is your preference. Jessie takes great pains to create an authentic environment, reminiscent of the Roaring Twenties.

When I arrived at *Jessie's* an hour later, I scanned the bar, then the tables, and recognized Samantha from her driver's license. She had on large sunglasses and sat toward the back. I walked over, introduced myself. She stood. We shook hands. Hers felt cold and as delicate as a child's.

"Thanks for coming so soon."

She looked to be about five feet tall, so my coat had to be way too big for her. Light brown hair framed a pretty face, lightly dusted with freckles.

We engaged in small talk for a while, and then I asked, "Why the shades?"

Her shoulders sagged. "I'd rather not talk about it."

I sighed. She had that look. The one that said the glasses were hiding a shiner and swollen eye.

"Hey, I'm sorry I don't mean to pry." I reached out to touch her hand, but she withdrew it.

I tried again. "Look Samantha, maybe I can help you. Has someone hit you?"

For a few long moments, neither of us spoke. Then she shook her head. "How can you possibly do anything to help?"

"Well, I provide counseling at the women's shelter, and teach self-defense. I have a second degree black belt in Tae Kwon Do, and run the kick boxing program at the Health and Fitness Club down the street. I give private lessons, and I am in demand as a personal trainer." I felt my face blush. I sounded like I was bragging, and I hate braggarts.

Samantha was staring at me. Then she took off her glasses. Her left eye was swollen and purple. "I'm not into fighting," she whispered.

Despite expecting the shiner, I was still shocked by the brutality of the assault. I remained calm, although I started to feel my anger boil up. "It's not so much fighting as it is strength, discipline, and confidence building. If you work with me, you may feel better, more self-assured, and in the future, you'll be able to defend yourself. Right now, I just want to make sure that you're OK."

She shrugged. "I'm OK."

I shook my head. "No. You're not OK. I know you're not OK because I've been a victim too."

I told her my story. "When I was younger, my dad often got drunk and hit my mom. When I tried to stop him, he smacked me around too. One day, I was so fed up that I grabbed a belt with a very large buckle, wrapped it around my hand and threatened to hit him in the eye. I told him that even if he hit me now, he would have to go to sleep sometime, and then I would beat him with my softball bat. Like most bullies, he backed off.

"He eventually got into counseling and stopped drinking, but I have never forgiven him for what he did to Mom. I haven't seen him since she died. She stayed with him until the end, and thankfully, he took decent care of her.

"A week after I stood up to him, I went to a local Tae Kwon Do school. Master Kim was standing by the entry door with his hands clasped behind him, watching the students. He was maybe about five-foot-six, but he had a commanding presence. He looked at each student as they warmed up. He knew I was there despite all the noise, and without moving, he asked me what I wanted. I asked if I could join his school.

"He turned to look at me. He saw the bruises on my arms. 'Who hit arms?'

'My dad.'

"His eyes widened and then narrowed. 'Father do this?' He shook his head in disbelief.

"I told him that I couldn't afford to go full time, maybe twice a week. He told me to pay him when I could and that I would be able to work off the monthly fee at the gym. He asked about my grades, and I told him that I had all A's.

"He wanted my mother to send a letter saying it was fine for me to work for him. He felt my determination and invited me in. He had a wonderful, kind face, and a twinkle in his eye that made him seem much younger than his seventy years, and much less dangerous than he actually was.

"I'll never forget that first day, his kindness. 'Then you here every day. No fail, understand? Now join group, run in place until I get there.'

"He was merciless because he had such high expectations of me. When he visited Korea, he had his boys push me harder than the other students. I could sense his chest swelling with pride as he wrapped the black belt around me. I made the grade faster than anyone except his sons. I became family and was often invited to his home for dinner. I helped his wife in the garden for hours, and we became close."

I looked down at the table. "He died two years ago from cancer. I miss him terribly."

Samantha whispered, "I don't have much money."

I wiped away a few tears and sat up straight. "It's on the house."

Her eyes widened. "Why?"

"Because, Samantha, you are exactly where I was fifteen years ago, and I don't want you to feel alone, the way I did. I guarantee that you will be transformed into a strong woman. Are you interested?"

She stared down at the table, then shook her head. "No, I'm not interested. At least not now."

I reached forward and gently grasped her hand. This time she didn't pull away. "You don't have to decide now. Here's my card. Call me when you're ready." I placed it in her hand and closed her fingers. We exchanged coats, but as she began to walk away, she stopped, then turned around and gave me a tentative hug.

"Call me anytime," I said. "Even if you only want to talk."

***

Six weeks sailed by. I thought of Sam often, and finally she called while I was at the gym.

"Melissa? This is Sam, Samantha Weiss?"

"Hey, Samantha Weiss. How are you?"

"Is it OK if I take you up on your offer?"

"Great! When can you start?"

"Uh, anytime?"

"Then come over now."

"I'm...I'm downstairs."

I stifled a laugh and invited her to my office.

A few minutes later she stood before me. The bruise had faded to a barely perceptible yellow. She was dressed in a dumpy pair of sweats that made her look twice as big as she was.

"You're going to fry in that. Are you wearing anything underneath?"

"Just my underwear."

"Oh, then you can take off the sweats after the work out, and sell memberships as the guys walk through."

She put her hands on her hips and looked at me in mock annoyance.

"Next time tank top and shorts, got it?"

"Yes, Master."

I was pleased at the sarcasm. She was less timid, always a good sign.

We did stretching and warm ups. Sam was panting after about fifteen minutes because she was in terrible shape.

"Can we take a break?" she asked.

"Nope. Let's go a half hour and then rest. Come on Weiss, don't be a wuss. This builds character."

"Dad told me that when he wanted me to take out the garbage."

"And?"

"I don't care about character."

***

Nine weeks later, her endurance had improved exponentially. Her hand-eye coordination was excellent, her kicks and punches were text book, and she was fast.

We worked out together three times a week for about two hours a session. Her need for breaks dwindled, but I made her stop to drink water and rest. She protested, but I wanted to avoid hyperthermia or dehydration for us both.

One day, while sparring in full padding, she feinted in one direction, and I dropped my guard; that was when she hit me in the face. Hard. I stopped, held my nose, and checked my glove. No blood. Then I glared at her. She was doing her footwork and smiling.

"That will never happen again."

"Come on, Williston. Don't be a wuss. Besides, your nose looks much better with that minor adjustment."

Sam hopped up and down, and tapped her gloves, motioning me forward. I pummeled her protective gear, but she laughed.

After our workouts, we usually went to *Jessie's Place*. Over the weeks that we'd worked out together, we were becoming good friends. It was a joy to watch Sam talk in a comfortable, animated way.

But one night she was unusually quiet.

"You OK?"

She stared at her hands, clenched and white-knuckled. "Mel, let me tell you about Richard. And the night that he hit me."

I nodded and felt my arms and shoulders tense. I waited.

"I met him when I was a junior accountant in the firm that worked for his family. He was brought in for me to review family financial information with him, because his father wanted Richard to have a grasp of all the books. He was a quick study, and we hit it off after spending time together at the office.

"He was handsome, with clear, bright green eyes and brown hair. His face was chiseled and ended in a lovely little cleft, my favorite part of him. He was about six feet tall and had a nicely muscled body.

"He took me to the best restaurants, and we often drove to his parents' summer home overlooking Lake Michigan. He was sweet, romantic, and attuned to my needs.

"He lived on the thirtieth floor of a lakefront high rise where we spent most of our evenings. I still kept my apartment and occasionally had some alone time there. Richard wanted me to move in with him, but I wanted to maintain my independence.

"He began to make iffy investments in the market and lost large amounts of money. That's when he started to change. Between the lost investments and my refusal to live with him, he became a different man.

"When he drank, he cursed at me, and sex was rougher. He hated that I was not totally under his control. A few days before you and I first met, he hit me.

"We had another argument over me not moving in. Out of nowhere, he slapped me so hard on the side of my face near my eye that I saw stars and a flash of light. The nausea became overwhelming, and I had a pounding headache.

"He had a shocked look on his face and tried to help me up. I shrugged him off and staggered out of the apartment. The doorman was worried about me, but when I refused an ambulance, he called a cab to take me to the ER. I was diagnosed with a concussion after a normal CAT scan.

"Richard was arrested, but was bailed out the next morning. After his mock trial he was slapped with fifty hours of community service due to his "clean" record. Big deal, right? His dad is wealthy, powerful, and knows a ton of people high up in city government, including judges.

"Of course, I was fired from the firm despite exemplary performance. My dad wanted me to fight it, but I didn't want to work there anymore. Now I work for my father's small firm, and I'm happy.

"Thankfully, I hadn't moved in with Richard. After the attack, I just took off, but I'd left behind several books that are signed first editions by my favorite authors."

The air was thick with despair. The story was all too common. Samantha was better off than most because she'd gotten out quickly and continued to work. He'd hit her, but she didn't have permanent physical damage, and she had a supportive family. And she'd turned herself around since we'd been working together.

"Wait a second," I exclaimed. "Why didn't Dr. Benson say anything while you were in his office, the day we switched coats?"

"I came in to get something for the nausea. I put my coat on the wall hook next to the check-in window and then realized that I'd left my wallet in the coat's pocket. As I turned, I noticed that his staff and some of the patients were staring at my bruised face. I felt so embarrassed that I left the office quickly and grabbed what I thought was my coat as I bolted from the waiting room."

***

One year after our first meeting, I waited for Sam at *Jessie's* to celebrate her milestone. She'd said she had to take care of some business first, but she'd be at Jessie's at our agreed time.

So I waited. I called her cell. No answer. Then I had a cup of tea. I texted her. No response. I grabbed a book from my backpack and tried to read, but couldn't concentrate. I called her again, but she didn't pick up. I was getting nervous. She was usually very punctual.

I kept looking at my watch. As I got up to leave and look for her, she blew into the restaurant like her little tornado self.

"Where the hell were you? I called, texted, but you didn't answer! I was worried sick!"

"Sorry. I went back to Richard's to get my stuff."

"You did what! You went without me to back you up?"

"I had to do it. It had been eating at me for weeks. I wanted my books so badly. I planned to get in and out quickly, just grab and go. I called his place from a pay phone, and when he didn't answer his landline, I assumed he was at work. I still had the key, so I went over, and let myself in.

"What made you think he hadn't changed the locks?"

"Why would he, Mel? I was never a threat to him. After all, he abused me."

"Good point. So what happened?"

"Unfortunately, he'd taken the day off. As I rifled through the bookshelf, the bedroom door opened behind me. He was as shocked to see me as I was to see him. He started yelling, 'Who do you think you are coming here? This is breaking and entering. You don't live here and you left me, remember?'

"I held up his keys and gently placed them on the dining room table next to the ugly silver candlesticks that his mother had given him. I told him I left him because he treated me like garbage, hit me, rang my bell big time, and put me in the ER. I told him it took weeks for me to fully recover, and I couldn't work. I told him that I didn't want any trouble, only a few books that had no value for him.

"He yelled at me to get out, and moved toward me.

"I faced him, holding my ground. He yelled, 'Are you serious?' Then he lunged.

"Every move he made was telegraphed, clumsy, and fueled by rage. He reeked of alcohol.

"I hit him with a left uppercut to the jaw, and as he turned, a right cross to the nose. It drew blood, and there was a satisfying crunch.

"Mel, you should have heard him scream! He yelled that I'd broken his nose, and he called me a bitch.

"He took a swing at me, but I ducked and my right hook struck his ribs. He dropped his guard, and I finished him off with a left roundhouse to the front of his chest. As he stumbled back, I shoved him hard against the buffet. He stood there, holding his nose to stop the bleeding, and looked at me.

"It was as if he saw who I was for the first time. I picked up one of the candlesticks and slapped the edge of the base in my open hand. I stared him down, and walked toward to him. His eyes practically popped out of his head with fear. He tried to speak, but stopped as I approached. He looked at the candlestick and swallowed hard.

"Mel, here's exactly what I said next. 'We're done, Richard. I promise that I will use this to put you in the hospital if you make the slightest move toward me. I want you to know that I showed enormous restraint in defending myself. I could have really hurt you, but I chose to have some class. Now go to your room and close the door until you hear me leave. You will find your mommy's candlestick at the base of the front stairs of the building. It's an insurance policy just in case you plan to ambush me. At some point, however, you should go to the ER because your nose is shifted to the right. Tell them that you fell so you can save face, no pun intended.

"'Now let me make this absolutely clear.' I pointed the candlestick directly at him for emphasis. 'We will never see each other again. If I even catch a glimpse of you in the future, I will put you in the hospital. Understand?'

"He walked to his bedroom, one hand on his nose and the other on his ribs, and closed the door. I took his prized top-of-the-line, high-grade leather gym bag, in exchange for my beat up pink one, and left."

Sam laughed. "You should have seen his face."

Our waitress had been wiping down the table next to us, very slowly. I knew she was listening to the story. Now we both stared at Sam, open-mouthed. Sam held up her hand and we high-fived. My face hurt from smiling so hard. I was so proud of her.

"Mel, thank you so much. You've turned me into a confident, fearless person. There will never be another Richard in my life again. Ever."

Our waitress came over to take our orders. Sam looked at her and said, "Now please tell me about tonight's special. All the ass-kicking has given me an appetite."

Carlos McReynolds
Encountering

Faint notes of tango drifted out from the dance hall as Mark stumbled out. Silvina leaned forward at the curb and raised her hand for a cab, a gesture which accentuated the skirt and heels she wore.

A gust of wind cooled his skin. He was sweaty from two hours of dancing. Silvina had claimed it was unseasonably cold for April in Buenos Aires. There was a moment of relief before he started shivering. He put on his coat.

"Mark." She turned to him. "I got one."

He stumbled a little as he followed her into the black and yellow taxi. His legs wobbled. He did not remember the last time he had danced so much. Even his coat seemed to hang strange.

The cab inside had the piney, chemical smell of cheap disinfectant, with a hint of cigarette smoke. Silvina and the driver exchanged a few sentences, in a cadenced Spanish of which Mark could only catch a few notes.

The car pulled away from the curb, and Silvina leaned back into her seat. She turned to Mark. "So, how did you like your first *milonga*?"

"I still don't know why you didn't let me bring a rose to hold in my teeth." He smiled.

She laughed. That was nice. He had tried that joke earlier, and she had given him a puzzled look.

"Oh, you." She laid her hand on his knee. "Such a silly affectation that would have been!"

"I just thought—well, there is a certain degree of costume to it. I've never seen you in heels that high or a skirt that short. I wonder what the people at the office would think."

She laughed. "Are you complaining, sweetie?"

He swallowed. "I—sorry, that was meant to be a joke."

She brought her other hand to his face. He could feel the cool spot on his cheek. She had kept her ring on.

"I had a good time," she continued. "I know you don't have much experience, but you did fine out there."

Her eyes scanned his face.

"I hope you're not jealous about me dancing with other men," she continued. "It's a *milonga*, a social dance. That is the expectation."

"As for my dress..." She smiled. "What's appropriate for Milwaukee may not be what's appropriate for a *milonga*."

"I'm sorry," he said. "I'm still a little tired. Between getting in last night, and—"

"I understand. We'll sleep in tomorrow."

Mark breathed a sigh of relief. He was finally on vacation with Silvina, far away from everything else.

The taxi had turned the last corner when a ringing filled its interior.

"I'm sorry." Silvina's hand came off of his cheek and grabbed her purse. She pulled out the little cell phone she had purchased that morning and brought it to her ear.

"*Hola, que contas?*"

Mark's first thought was that it might be Chad. No, she continued in Spanish, and she never spoke to Chad in Spanish.

The call lasted a few minutes. The cab arrived at the front of the building, but Silvina signaled to the driver to wait one moment.

"I'm so sorry, sweetie," she said while she dug in her purse. She pulled out several bills, which she handed to the driver. "That was my cousin Alejandra. There's a family situation. I have to go out to San Luis tonight."

"You have to—but why tonight?" Mark stammered. "Would— why not just go in the morning?"

"If I leave in the next ten minutes, I can meet Alejandra at Retiro, and we can get on a bus that will get us there by the morning. I have enough time to grab some things for the trip."

They were already walking up the stairs before he thought to say anything else.

"Why don't I come with you?" he suggested. "I can get stuff together and take the bus too."

"Oh, sweetie, that wouldn't be a good idea. It will only be a day or two, and I'll be right back."

"You were going to show me the city. You know how bad my Spanish is."

"I'm sure you'll find plenty to do. We get lots of tourists here. Just try to enjoy yourself."

Mark stood by the door, just inside the apartment. Her mind was made up, but he wished he could say something to keep her from leaving. Finally, he surrendered to the circumstance.

He took off his coat to start getting ready for bed, but in the light of the apartment, he saw now that it was not the coat he had put on when they went out. It was a black wool coat, just like his, and the general outline was much the same, but the lines seemed a little cleaner, the stitching a little tighter. He glanced at the label and saw an unfamiliar Italian name. Custom made, perhaps?

"Silvie," he called out to her as she dashed from the bathroom to the bedroom, open overnight bag in hand. "This isn't my coat."

"What's that?" She poked her head out from the bedroom.

"The coat check girl gave me the wrong coat."

"Call the hall tomorrow." She walked towards him, overnight bag now closed. "Is his *cedula* is in there? Maybe you can find the owner yourself."

"*Cedula?*"

"His ID." She looked at her watch. "I have to go. I hope the driver is still down there. I'll call you tomorrow and let you know how things are going."

She lifted herself up on her toes and kissed his cheek. "I hope you have a good time."

After she left, Mark stood holding the coat. A feeling of exhaustion came over him. He threw the coat on the back of one of the dining room chairs and went to bed.

***

Mark awoke the next day, his arm resting across the empty space on the bed. He got up and shuffled to the kitchen. When he got there, he realized he had been expecting Silvina to prepare breakfast.

He sat at the dining room table. His eyes scanned the room, as if there were some hint amidst the furniture and photos, and fell on the thick, black coat folded over the back of a dining room chair. The coat that wasn't his.

He picked it up, seeing once again the unfamiliar Italian name on the inside. He looked through the pockets, searching for some clue to the owner's identity.

When he was done, all of the contents sat on the dining room table: a brown leather wallet, an envelope from the Hotel Zorzal, three one-peso coins, a box of cards, and a cheap-looking cell phone.

The phone was an ugly rectangular item with raised buttons. No calls or pictures or emails. The only message said: *45. La reunión. El agua está sobre la tierra. El rey se aproxima al templo.* It didn't make much sense—something about a reunion and water and a king? Or did *reunión* mean meeting? What was that old saying? Journeys end in strangers meeting—or something like that.

The cards were decorated with a curious emblem: a yellow disk with spears coming out and a crown on top. They must have been Spanish playing cards—*naipes*, as Silvie called them.

The hotel envelope had two key cards and a room number. The wallet had several hundred peso bills and a Uruguayan ID for a man named Georges Umbral. Who would leave their wallet and room keys in a coat they were checking?

The obvious next step was to call the hotel, talk to the man or leave him a message. Mark had never cared for the phone. You couldn't pick up body language, look a person in the eye, size him up. He laughed. How well would his high school Spanish hold up when all he had to go on was a voice?

He put the coat on over his pajamas and walked into the bedroom, facing the dresser mirror. It would be wrong to hold on to this coat, of course.

He held out his hand to his reflection.

"Hello," he said. "That is a fine looking coat you're wearing."

He smiled, made as if shaking hands.

"I am Georges Umbral." He added a little bit of an accent to his voice, and gave the first G that hard *zh* Argentines used when they said a word with a y or a double-l. "I have this crazy story to tell you about how a gringo wound up with my coat."

No, it wouldn't do at all. Holding on to this coat. The best thing would be to go right over to the hotel and explain to the hotel clerk, or to Mr. Umbral, if he was available. It would be easier to explain in person, coat in hand. That would be the thing to do. He put the coat down, showered, and got dressed.

He grabbed some of the cash he had withdrawn the day before, slipping it and the apartment keys into his jeans pocket.

He put on the coat and headed into the street, and while looking for a taxi, noticed the Starbucks on the corner. It was a relief to see a familiar brand. He satisfied himself with two muffins and a latte.

He managed to flag down a cab and communicate the name of the hotel to the driver. As the cab wove its way towards the center of the city, it passed a park. On the other side of the park was a wide low building, a tall green cupola extending upwards from its center.

"*Que es eso?*" Mark extended his hand towards the strange building.

"*El Congreso,*" the cabbie replied.

Mark thought it looked like a malformed copy of the Capitol building, stripped of its skin, revealing a gray and green skeletal structure. What he had seen so far of the city left a similar impression, a copy of a European city, with an element of it removed, naked in its greyness.

The door to the hotel, situated at the intersection of two streets, had a dramatic brass frontispiece of shields, swords, suns and stars.

The lobby was even more elegant than the door in front had suggested. The marble floors and brass fittings were old, but somehow the years had buffed them to a kind of timelessness. How much would it cost to stay in a place like this?

He walked to the marble-topped front desk, where a tall, thin man spoke to him in an attentive Spanish. Mark caught only a few words. He had prepared nothing in response.

"*Si... por favor...,*" he spluttered, before blurting out. "*Señor Umbral.*"

"*Por supuesto,*" said the clerk, giving an almost imperceptible nod. He turned and took a few steps away, looking through a folder. When he came back, he had an envelope.

Before Mark could say anything else, the clerk held out the envelope and said a few words.

Mark reached for it and took it. Had Mr. Umbral left a message for him? Mark opened the envelope and removed a sheet of thick, creamy paper. He struggled to read the words written in black cursive. They were Spanish. He understood very little of it, but there was no mention of a coat.

He looked up at the clerk and back towards the note. It had been intended for the owner of the coat, not the man returning it. The clerk eyed him, expectant.

Mark wondered what to do. He'd look pretty stupid now, or as if he were trying to impersonate a guest.

"*Algo mas?*" asked the clerk.

"*No, uh, gracias—no mas,*" said Mark.

It would be easier just talking to Mr. Umbral. He'd understand this was all a simple mix-up. Even if the man was absent, Mark had the hotel room's key cards. He could just switch the coats, set things right himself. He looked at the little envelope and found the room number.

There were only two elevators. Even with the door closed he could see into them, cast iron curlicues of petrified ivy the only barrier between the riders and the empty space beyond.

Mark floundered for a few minutes with the doors, which had to be opened and closed by hand, first the outer and then the inner, in order to get in and make the elevator move.

The room was located near the end of a long hallway. A tag hung from the door, likely a "Do Not Disturb" message. Mr. Umbral was probably there, possibly sleeping. He might not want to be bothered, but this should only take a second.

Mark formulated the few phrases he would need to explain. His grammar may not be perfect, but Mr. Umbral would get his meaning.

He knocked. Several long moments passed with no response. Maybe Umbral still slept and could only hear knocking in his dreams.

Mark thought about knocking again. He couldn't just stand there. How would that look?

He pulled out the message from the clerk. He could write something on it, slip it under the door, go to the lobby for a little while. Or the note might give some indication of Mr. Umbral's whereabouts.

He read over the first line again.

Georges, o lo que sea tu nombre...

The words looked familiar, but he was not sure of their meaning. Something about a name, suggesting uncertainty.

...no entiendo tu juego, pero no pienso venir.

Something about a game, and something that was not true or not happening. *Pienso* had to do with belief or thought, but *venir* he could not find within his memories.

La venganza...

Venganza—a word he had never forgotten. It stuck in the brain, redolent of blood and fury. Vengeance. What was beyond that door?

The lock clicked. A crack of light shone where the door began to open. Mark brought the message down into his pocket where he had put the pack of cards.

In the open doorway stood a man, his hands tucked into a white hotel robe. The man stood eye-to-eye with Mark. They had the same widow's peak of dark hair, though Mr. Umbral's was fuller and healthier.

"You're early," said the man in the doorway. The accent was unfamiliar.

"I—were you expecting me?"

"Why don't you come inside? I'll order us some coffee."

"I think there's a misunderstanding here—"

"You really look like you could use a coffee." The man in the doorway pulled his right hand from the robe's pocket, revealing it gripped a pistol.

Mark looked down the empty hall. How far could he make it? Would the man risk killing him here? It was just a simple mix-up. Surely, someone else was the target of this man's displeasure.

"I guess it would be ungracious of me to refuse." Mark smiled.

The man now backed away from the doorway. He waited until Mark had entered to lock the door behind him.

Luxurious crimson couches lined the near walls, a glass-topped coffee table in front of each. A marble bar stood near the entrance, a familiar black coat draped across it. Mark could see nine cards laid out in a pattern on one of the coffee tables.

"You see." The man gestured toward the cards. "I've been trying to determine your fate."

"Does it include coffee?"

The man laughed. "We will find out together."

He waved Mark over to the table. Two rows—six cards—had been flipped over. Three remained face down. "You see, I've seen only your past and present. I thought we might learn your future together."

The backs of the cards had a familiar shield and crown logo. Where had he seen that before? Mark pulled the deck from his coat pocket. The man barely moved in response, his eyes narrowing until he saw the cards.

"I see you came prepared." The man smiled. "You think you know my destiny?"

Mark looked at the cards and back at the man with the gun. Was the man just toying with him?

"N-nine cards, right?" This was crazy, but maybe it would buy him a couple of minutes. "Three each; past, present and future?"

The man nodded. Mark worried his hands would shake too much, but he was able to shuffle the cards and lay down nine of them.

There had to be a way to buy more time.

"You haven't told me what the cards tell you," Mark said. "What do you see in my past?"

The man gestured towards the first row. A king held his hand out to a floating grail. A knight on warhorse held a club—not a funny little clover, but a rough wooden weapon. Four daggers plunged inwards.

"Not much there. Only child. Wasted potential. The usual disappointments. Can't say as I envy your alimony payments."

Mark nodded, hating to admit how true it all sounded. He flipped over the first row of the cards he had dealt. He saw the king with the grail, the knight and his weapon, the four blades. How was that possible?

Mark bluffed. "Do you need me to tell you what they say?"

"There's nothing there I didn't already know," the man replied. He gestured towards the next row of cards. Six swords arranged in two rows, like jagged teeth. An androgynous figure making a toast with another grail. Six fat goldfish crowded together—no, those must be clubs.

"You're keeping secrets." The man shrugged. "You're here with someone you shouldn't be. You're not as important to her as you thought you were."

Mark flinched. That had to be a lucky guess.

If it had been less grim, he would have laughed at this demented game of nine-card stud. That would have been better. He would have had a chance if it was poker.

The man gestured. "It's your turn."

Mark flipped over the next row: six swords, the man or woman with a cup, the six fat clubs. What if the man thought it was a trick?

"Does that look about right?" Mark had no idea what it meant.

The man glanced over the cards and shrugged. "We're even now."

"We could go at the same time," Mark blurted out. This couldn't be done already, could it?

The man glanced up, then flipped over his last three cards.

Three golden coins, a robed king clutching a club twice the size of the knight's, eight swords making up an even more wicked mouthful of teeth.

For the first time, Mark saw the man with the gun hesitate. The cards seemed to confuse him.

Before anything else could happen, Mark flipped over the last row of his draw, not even looking at them. The man flinched and stared up straight at Mark, looking as if he had unexpectedly busted at blackjack. Mark could see the anger play on his features.

"Maybe I should go." He began to move towards the door.

The man kicked the table over, sending both decks flying. Mark stumbled back. The man jumped over the table, the gun now out of the robe pocket. He grabbed Mark's coat lapels with his free hand and backed him towards the door.

"What makes you think you're right? Why should I care what they have to say?"

"They're your cards, your coat," Mark blurted out.

"My—how did you? Who—"

It had caught the man off guard. Seeing his confusion, Mark pushed off with his legs. The two of them fell back towards the bar. The countertop struck the man in the small of the back. The gun jerked from his hand and slid under a couch.

The man fell to the floor, the wind apparently knocked out of him, but Mark managed to stay on his feet. Mark turned towards the door, removing the coat as he did so.

It was only a few steps, during which he feared a shot would come. Instead, he only heard the other man mutter, "No, it can't be."

He did not look back as he turned the lock, threw the coat on the floor and shot out the door. He ran past the elevator to a stairwell, taking the stairs as fast as his body would allow. He stumbled out the door into the lobby, where he leaned against a wall to catch his breath. The employees eyed him suspiciously, but didn't bother him when he ran outside.

It had started to rain while he was inside. The drops felt cold and sharp on his bare skin.

What had that been about?

He ran, weaving around people. They muttered in annoyance as he raced by.

He collapsed, wet and shivering, in the park behind which loomed the green cupola of *El Congreso*.

He felt the keys in his pocket. He hoped he would be safe back in the empty apartment.

If only he could keep running, past the outskirts of the city, away from the press of buildings and the proximity of humanity. Leave it behind. Leave it all behind.

He gripped the keys in his hand. A quick throw sent them off into a bush.

He turned towards where he imagined north would be. It would have been a warm day back home.

A cold breeze bore down on him. He wrapped his arms around himself and shivered.

Cindy Wallach
Slicker Swap

Yesterday when I woke up,
I sneezed once or twice.
The sky was grey and gloomy,
So Mom gave me advice.
"Looks like rain," she told me.
"I don't want you getting sicker.
So here, put on this sweater,
And you better take your slicker."

My slicker is a raincoat
That's made of yellow plastic.
None of my friends wear them,
But I think mine's fantastic!
I got mine two years ago
When I was pretty small.
And now that I am growing,
It doesn't fit at all.

So I decided I would bring
My slicker, wear my sweater.
The sweater keeps me warm,
But they are just too tight together.
The kids at school all wore their coats.
Boots were everywhere.
So I kept on my sweater and
Put my slicker on a chair.

That was okay, and through the day
I never thought about it.
So I guess it's no surprise
That I went home without it.
"Oh no!" I yelped. "My slicker!
I left it on the chair!"
I whipped around and ran back,
But my slicker wasn't there.

Cindy Wallach

Disaster! It's gone! Where is it!
I searched everywhere:
In the closets, in the drawers,
Under rugs and up the stairs.
When suddenly a mom appeared
Looking worried, walking quicker.
"Excuse me," she said and held it up.
"Is this your yellow slicker?"

Hooray! Hooray! My slicker!
"Thank you! I'm so glad!
I was afraid I lost it.
My mom would be so mad."
"We've got a family slicker too.
My older children shared it.
My youngest says it's his turn now,
But he's too small to wear it."

In walked her son! I knew 'cause he wore
A great big yellow slicker!
"Mom, this coat's gigantic!
I trip when I walk quicker!"
"No prob," I said. "Mine's too small,
But it should fit him right.
Wanna use it? I can't wear
A slicker that's too tight!"

"Let's slicker swap!" his mother said.
"The perfect way to do it!
You can always work it out
When you muddle through it."
I put on his coat, it fit just fine,
No reason to complain!
"This is great! We both have coats
To wear home in the rain!"

Bonny Kotapish
Misconception

Clare looked up from her grocery list as Clyde barked by the back door.

"Okay, just let me get a coat. I don't have fur to keep me warm," she told him as she went to the closet.

"Oh, darn, stupid light bulb—whose coat do I have? Oh, Elyse's will work."

Clare slipped her arms in her daughter's coat and snapped the top. She opened the door and followed the dog out.

"Hurry up, I'm freezing!" Clare yelled to Clyde while she closed more snaps. She shoved her hands in the pockets of the coat, and felt around for some gloves. Instead, her hand hit something hard with a bag around it. She pulled it out and squinted at it in the setting sun. Her heart sank to the frozen ground. Clyde bounded back, oblivious to the chaos spinning through Clare's mind as she turned toward the house.

Clare dropped into the kitchen chair, unable to think of anything except the used pregnancy test she had just discovered in her daughter's coat pocket. Now that she was in better lighting, she could see the little blue plus sign indicating she was going to be a grandmother—much sooner than she had ever thought.

Elyse had come home from school subdued, but she was seventeen—her moods weren't always predictable and the reasons weren't always shared. Obviously, there were many things Elyse didn't share with her anymore. She hadn't even told Clare that she was seeing anyone!

How could Clare be so blind? How was she going to screw up the courage to have this talk with her? It had to be done, but what would she say? Clare wasn't prepared for this. They'd talked about so many things, even this possibility and how it would change everything: sleepless nights, the difficulty of continuing school, no money.

Clare had really thought Elyse got it.

Jacob, Clare's son, came into the kitchen to grab a snack, completely unaware of her turmoil. He was home for the holidays from his first college semester.

Jacob got it. He'd gotten through high school without the drama. He'd had a steady girlfriend for two years, Madison. He'd met her at Elyse's 15th birthday party. She and Elyse would be graduating together in the spring. Now it looked like Elyse would be walking up the ramp with a baby bump! Clare's head reeled. Her stomach turned.

Jacob went back to the family room. Clare stood and climbed the stairs to Elyse's room.

She steadied herself, knocked on the door and called her daughter's name.

"C'mon in." Elyse turned down her iPod as her mother entered the room.

"Elyse, we need to talk. I used your coat to take out Clyde and found this in the pocket. Do you have anything to tell me?"

Clare's trembling palm opened. Her daughter's face paled.

"Mom, d-don't lose it! It's not m-mine! I swear!" stammered Elyse.

Clare crossed her arms and lowered her chin. "Please, don't make this worse by lying. How could you do this? How could you be so irresponsible?"

"Mom, please!"

"Who's the father? How long have you known? You haven't even finished high school! How will you raise this baby?

Elyse exhaled.

"Mom, slow down. I'm not lying. It's a friend's. I'm holding on to it for her. She was afraid her parents would find it! She didn't want to tell them until the father knew and they could tell both their parents together. Mom! Honest!"

"Why wouldn't your friend keep it in her pocket? Really, Elyse, trust me and just tell the truth. We'll get through it and deal with it, but tell the truth!"

"*You* found it in *my pocket!* Please! Listen to me! She was so paranoid that it would fall out. Mom, I can't say anything except that it is the truth. I learned my lesson after you caught me sneaking out. I wouldn't lie about something like this!"

"Then who is your 'friend'?"

"I can't tell you. She hasn't even told the father yet! I swore I'd keep her secret."

Jacob came into the room. He had heard the raised voices and, naturally, had listened to the conversation.

"Oh-oh, Elyse, did I hear right? Are you preggers?"

"No, I'm not, Jacob. And I don't want to talk about it."

"Jacob, I'll talk to you later." Clare rubbed her temples. "Please, go downstairs. I need to talk to your sister. Alone."

Her son leaned on the door jamb and crossed his arms. "No way, Mom! This is going to affect everyone in the family! How could you do this, Elyse? What are people going to say about us? I would never be so stupid!"

"Jacob, it is *not* my pregnancy test! I have never taken one and I have never had a reason to take one!"

"Oh, so immaculate conception, huh?"

Clare threw up her hands. "Jacob, you are not helping. Leave your sister alone. I don't know what to believe. I'm going downstairs. Elyse, I'll leave you to think about all of this."

Jacob scowled and shook his head. "How can you let her off so easy? This is such a dumbass mistake!"

"Jacob, this is between Elyse and me for now. Elyse, I expect that if you are not being honest, you'll come to your senses. Besides it will show soon enough. If you aren't trying to pull the wool over my eyes, then I guess I would be proud of you for being a good friend, but I certainly don't like the circumstances." Clare put the white plastic lightning rod on Elyse's desk. "I'll leave this here."

Jacob waited for his mother to leave the room, then turned on Elyse.

"It's not yours? Bull! You just don't want to admit being pregnant! How could you be so irresponsible?! You just shot your future in the foot!"

"Jacob, shut up!" Elyse balled her fists.

"Where are you going to fit this kid? You were always so fussy about your room—don't touch this, don't touch that—don't put that there. Eeew, you'll get it dirty! Man, are you in for a change! And I am going to laugh!"

"I am not that stupid! I don't have to worry about where I'll put it or how I'll raise it! I told you I do not want to talk about it! And especially not with you!"

"Why not me? C'mon, I'm your big brother. I do believe I have someone's butt to kick if he doesn't do the right thing and back you up. And Dad is gonna freak when he finds out."

"For the last time, Jacob—it's NOT MINE! I can't talk to you about it, *please*!"

"I'll tell you the same thing Mom did. The truth will show soon enough. And when you look like a Goodyear blimp, I'm taking pictures."

"You..." Elyse flung a pillow at her brother.

"I don't know, when it comes down to it, maybe it'll be fun being an uncle, seeing you walk around sleep-deprived, with baby food on your shirt."

"No more, Jacob! It's not like I don't have any ammunition I could use against you!" Elyse stood and grabbed the test stick. "Keep it up and I'm gonna stick this up...."

Downstairs, the doorbell rang.

"All right, all right! I gotta go. Madison wanted to see me as soon as I got back, and we're going out to dinner and a movie."

Jacob went to get his coat from the family room where he'd dropped it. As he did, Elyse came down to say hi to his girlfriend and give her a hug.

Jacob brushed his hand across Elyse's shoulder on his way out and whispered, "Listen, Leecy. I still can't believe you were this dumb. But seriously, I guess it will be okay. I will be there for you. We'll talk later. At least, I'm home so you don't have to face Mom and Dad alone." He gave her a gentle noogie as he walked past.

Jacob and Madison walked down the front walk together. As he opened the car door, Madison looked back. Elyse waved from the front window, wondering how it was going to feel to be an aunt.

John Quinn
Pink

Men and women are different. They are different in mind as well as body. The shape and function of each gender's fleshy parts are well documented by scientific tome, in parental handbooks, and grainy film. The shape and function of the brain, especially the left lobe, is where the difference lies.

A woman sees nuances and connections in objects and qualities that would no more occur to a man than unaided flight.

For instance, when a woman says *white*, she means ivory with a hint of blue, something that will go with the sofa and accent the drapes. What the man hears is the name of a color that looks like milk, two percent or whole, it doesn't matter. As long as it's not chocolate, it's *white*!

This was brought home to me as my wife and I prepared the house for our first child. We were expecting a girl. Our expectations were based not on some pseudo-science involving cameras, doctors, and electricity, but rather on that magical part of the left brain called woman's intuition.

"My mother had three girls. My grandmother had five girls. I am going to have a girl."

We proceeded with our preparations and plans accordingly.

The child-to-be was named. It was not the name I would have chosen. (I wanted to name her after one of her grandmothers; that way monogrammed stuff would be passed on to her.) My wife wanted the baby to be christened Gliven, after some soap opera diva. The godparents she chose were Art and Bill, a gay couple we played bridge with. My sister and my wife's brother were too "ordinary." Our daughter was to be special!

And, of course, because our she was to be a she, everything must be tinted pink.

Our mutual problem arose when we decided to paint the nursery. I, personally, thought of that room as my office, but that was before the influx of fragile pink furniture. There was the pink-sheeted crib, changing station, rocking chair with the cute pink bunnies dabbed into the varnish, and, of course, the pink dresser.

One Thursday, three months prior to our due date, I had the day off of work. As she left for her own job, (me still in my pajamas, sipping coffee and reading the sports page), my wife said so sweetly, touchingly, sort of pleadingly, "Could you paint the nursery?"

Without looking up, I, unwittingly said, "Sure."

"Pink."

"What?" I responded.

"Pink, we want the walls and ceiling pink."

"Of course," I snorted. "What else?"

She paused. I looked up. She seemed to want to say something, but thought better of it, blew me a kiss, and was gone.

After another cup of coffee, I drove to the paint store. I selected two brushes that would do the job, a roller and a paint tray, and, of course, a drop cloth for the floor.

This was not the first coat of paint in my life.

And then it came to paint.

A sedate, elderly gentleman was guiding me through the aisles. "Color?"

"Pink." The moment I said pink, I saw some gray hairs on the back of his neck wiggle, as if they wanted to get away.

He stopped and turned, hands clenched at his sides, head cocked to his left. I had recently read about dogs: when their tails wag on the right, they want to be friends; tails wagging on the left is a sign of fear or aggression.

I sensed fear or aggression from the clerk.

"Do you have something more definite?" He was smiling, but I could tell his tail was still wagging left. "We have twenty-seven shades of pink." His hand quivered as he pulled out a sheet of pink tones.

'What's the matter?" I realized he was afraid. "Did I say something wrong?"

"No! No!" He looked up with the saddest eyes. "It's just that men should never be sent to pick pink anything.

"I don't understand." And I didn't.

"Pink is a beautiful color, and when it comes to sunsets and distant mountains, men can comment." He shuddered. "But when it comes to wall paint..." His voice trailed to a moan.

With some trepidation on his part and a growing unease on mine, we decided on a pink that we both thought might be the least objectionable.

It took me four hours, two pots of coffee, and seven chocolate cookies, but the room was painted before my wife got home from work.

The pink-sheeted crib, the changing station, the rocking chair with the cute pink bunnies, and the pink dresser were piled neatly in the living room. The house was filled with the unmistakable scent of fresh paint. I was in the kitchen with coffee and my eighth cookie when my wife got home.

My grin was satisfaction and anticipation.

"What did you do!" She was standing in the doorway to the nursery. "What in God's name have you done?"

She turned towards me. Her face twisted with anger and tears.

"It clashes with everything! Wrong color! Wrong texture! Wrong coat!"

I was devastated. To me, pink is pink. "I'll do it again. We can do it again. Together!"

"Damn right, together." Her pretty little fists were tight, knuckles white, flesh red. Her face, the face I love, was twisted in a pink and white mask more appropriate to that moment when the heroine finally confronts the serial killer. Except there was no spooky music, just silence.

Soon came Saturday. We went to the paint store together. I just hoped the sedate, elderly gentleman would do no "I told you so" dance, but he was polite and helpful as she and he (mostly she) conferred on the aesthetic and practical values of various shades of pink.

I assumed he had forgotten his experience with me two days ago, but as he handed me a receipt for two gallons of Sunrise Pink flat paint, he patted my hand and rendered a sympathetic nod.

I spent a second day painting away all vestiges of my office, my past life, and the wrong coat of pink. The love of my life would occasionally appear in the doorway and stare at me with her arms crossed and her jaw set.

The next day, I moved the pink furniture back into the room. We were ready for Gliven.

But, as fortune would have it, genetics be damned. We had a boy. She named him James, after her maternal grandfather.

I had the room painted blue, an inoffensive shade of Little-Boy Blue (honest, that was what the label said). The pink sheets were in the attic before she and Baby James got home from the hospital.

Art and Fred were godparents as Bill had given up on Art and bridge. Bill was now into Samuel and pinochle.

And it turned out just the way most fairy tales turn out. We had two more children, both girls, and I was a lot better prepared the second and third time.

Barry Abrams, "Redemption"

Barry Abrams is a pediatrician and urgent care physician with thirty-five years of experience. He started writing five years ago after he attended a narrative writing workshop at his thirty-year medical school reunion. He integrates humor into his practice and feels that when patients experience the joy of laughter, they can overcome the adversity of illness. He began his writing career with humor pieces such as "Flying Tennis Balls" and "In a Pig's Eye" which were published in www.oakparkjournal.com. He has since begun writing poetry and medically themed essays. After caring for battered women in his practice, he chose to write a piece for *The Wrong Coat* anthology that represented an amalgam of the women he has treated over the years, and the redemption that they collectively earned after their abusers were confronted and vanquished.

Marie Anderson, "Coat Check"

Marie Anderson is a married mother of three living in La Grange, IL. She is the founder and facilitator of the La Grange Library Writers Group. During the school year, she helps supervise and "entertain" five hundred grade school children during their lunch recess. Her stories and essays have appeared in various publications, including *Brain Child, St. Anthony Messenger, Woman's World, Downstate Story*, and *Writer's Digest*. In 2012, she was a finalist in *The Great American Think-Off* essay/debate competition. Her hobbies are knitting, playing Scrabble, decluttering, and tidying.

Contributors

Sally Anderson, "To Tell the Truth"

Sally Anderson has lived in the La Grange, IL area all her life. She holds a BA in Communications from Northern Illinois University and a Master of Business Administration from Benedictine University. She has always had a love for writing. Her first published piece, a poem about Molly Pitcher, appeared in her junior high school literary magazine. She has worked on the Triton College newspaper and has also served several years as writer and editor of *The Voice*, her church newsletter. In addition to writing and reading, her favorite hobby is trying out new recipes. She is currently working on finishing her first novel.

Janet Barrett, "Pocketful"

Janet Barrett explores the possibilities of her imaginative fiction, poetry, and creativity in her "no-spare time." A former journalist, she has produced hundreds of newspaper and online articles, feature stories, personality profiles, press releases, and a ton of e-mails. She currently works as a desktop publishing specialist.

Jim Chmura, "Best in Plaid"

Jim Chmura's favorite fiction format is the short story. He tends towards fantasy, although his ventures into horror and science fiction are not unusual. His ten years as a stringer for a suburban Chicago newspaper taught him the economy of words. He was nominated in 2010 for *The Pushcart Prize in Fiction* for his humorous short story concerning an elderly man's argument with the Grim Reaper. In 2015, his short story about a young artist's betrayal by his most trusted friend was published in *The Chicago Tribune's Printers Row Journal*. Born and raised in the Pilsen area of Chicago, he attributes the grit of his Chicago stories to his childhood days. Currently residing in Oak Park, IL, he is semi-retired and continues his endless wrestling match with the printed word.

Kevin M. Folliard, "Polar Bound"

Kevin M. Folliard is a La Grange, IL fiction writer with a degree in English and creative writing from the University of Illinois in Urbana-Champaign. His published fiction includes the scary story collections *Christmas Terror Tales* and *Valentine Terror Tales*, and three adventure novels for ages twelve and up: *Jake Carter & the Nightmare Gallery*, *Violet Black & the Curse of Camp Coldwater*, and *Jimmy Chimaera & the Temple of Champions*. Folliard's work has been collected in *Sanitarium Magazine*, as well as in anthologies by Nosetouch Press and Black Bed Sheet Books. You can learn more about his writing at www.KevinFolliard.com.

Lorelei Glaser, "Mea Culpa"

Lorelei Glaser lived in Chicago until she married and moved to the northern suburbs. After reading Betty Friedan's book, *The Feminine Mystique*, she had an epiphany, enrolled in Mundelein College, and earned a teaching degree. She taught special education in the public and private sectors. She is an accomplished watercolorist, and also participates in current event and book discussion groups. Activities that bring her most joy are those she shares with her children and grandchildren. She did not choose to write – it chose her. She believes the human condition is the writer's inspiration.

Linda Lea Graziani, "Fifi and Madame"

Linda Lea Graziani, a fiction writer based in the Chicago area, was inspired to write "Fifi and Madame" by her experiences in sketch writing classes at The Second City. She is also the author of *The Molly Chronicles*. This humorous novelette series includes: *I, Sofa*; *I, Illumination*; *I, Rugart*; and *I, Molly*. These novelettes center on the adventures of a young woman named Molly and her perplexing romantic interest in eye-catching furniture. Meanwhile, Molly's awkward but sincere neighbor, Eric, tries desperately to change her notions of what love can be. Linda Lea has a B.A. in Social Sciences. She feels that her studies in sociology, humanities, and psychology have helped her create realistic and complex characters. The author is aware that Fifi and Madame may beg to differ with the previous statement. All novelettes are available for download from Amazon.com.

Judith Kessler, "Coat Thief"

Judith Filek Kessler grew up nurtured in art and creativity. She wrote and illustrated a children's story about America for a German exchange teacher while he taught at Ripon High School in Wisconsin. She was a student in the liberal arts program at Ripon College, earned a Court Reporting Degree in Madison, Wisconsin, and studied at DePaul University in Chicago. She works as an RRT in the respiratory field. Her published writing includes articles in *Respiratory Tract*, a children's story, "The Frightful Storm," in *Life News Magazine*, and editorials in local newspapers. She's been a member of SCBWI since 1996, attends writing seminars and workshops, and is active with the La Grange Library Writers Group. She lives to draw and write for a better world with her stories and poems. Her goal is to encourage and support positive attributes and experiences for children and teens. Currently she is looking to publish elephant stories and poems for personal discovery and wellbeing. She can be found enjoying lakes, nature, and natural habitats whenever possible.

Bonny Kotapish, "Misconception"

Bonny Kotapish is a married mother of three and grandmother of two. She lives in La Grange Park, IL and works as a caregiver. Her main writing interests are family and animals.

Carlos McReynolds, "Encountering"

Carlos McReynolds has wanted to be a writer since he was very young growing up in South Florida. After living on the West Coast for the better part of a decade, he moved to the Chicago area about three years ago, where he is employed as a data mining analyst, helping state workforce agencies combat and prevent fraud. He has been interested in weird fiction since discovering the works of H.P. Lovecraft in his early twenties.

Joan Nelson, "Mistake"

Joan Nelson is a picture book writer with an art background and two previous art-related businesses, The Tin Works and Cloud 9. Joan began writing after joining Off Campus Writer's Workshop in Winnetka, IL, and SCBWI. She is grateful to now be part of the La Grange Library Writers Group and continues writing quirky characters, humor, as well as surprise endings. Joan has taught art to elementary school children in park district programs, at the Chicago Northside Girls and Boys Club, and to homeschooled children. She has drawn for the Chicago Junior League's *Topics Magazine*, *Rhino*, *Review of Poetry and Short Prose*, and for advertisements for The Little Bookstore in Hinsdale, IL. "Mistake" is the first attempt Joan has made to tell a story through rhyme. She has always been encouraged by her husband, three daughters, and ten grandchildren.

Ruth Princess, "The Michelin Man"

Ruth J. Princess began writing as personal therapy journaling. A decade after recording her weight-loss trials and tribulations, she learned writing skills from the La Grange Library Writers Group. Along with honing her humor through Toastmasters, she published a self-help book. *Diary of a Fat Female* is not a diet book but rather a story-filled eating guide. Ruth firmly believes that to achieve your goals, you need to write them down. Writing "The Michelin Man" for *The Wrong Coat* anthology motivated Ruth to finally leave the cold northern winters and move to sunny Florida. Learn more about her at youtube.com/user/ruthejp13 or purchase her books at Amazon.com.

John Quinn, "My Jacket, Oh My Jacket" and "Pink"

John Quinn is one of the elders. He has lived (with the same woman) in Brookfield, IL for over forty years, has two accomplished daughters, and is a graduate of the University of Notre Dame. He is retired from IBM. John writes poetry, some short fiction, and nonfiction in which he attempts humor. He follows Chicago sports teams (excluding the Cubs) and Notre Dame football. Besides writing, he reads a lot, naps a lot, and waits for something to happen. It's the napping and waiting he does best. He is a member of three writing groups and two poetry groups, and a past president of the Illinois State Poetry Society. His poems have been published in a number of collections.

Margo Rife, "Hang in There, Hamlet"

Margo's theatrical journey began with Back Door Theater in La Grange, IL where her son acted in three productions. Margo used her graphic arts background to help with set design. Encouraged by the creative director, she began to write a few scenes. Soon Margo was hooked and wrote a full-length play titled *A Whale of a Tale* that was staged at The Reber Center in La Grange. With script in hand, Margo signed up for the *Play in Progress Class* at Chicago Dramatists. As a Network Playwright with CD, she had a scene from *Once in a Whale* presented in their *Showcase of Student Plays*. Margo is a member of Theatre of Western Springs Playwriting Group and La Grange Writers Group. She is developing a play with LGWG called *Ex Libris* about the last library in America. Margo hopes to expand *Hang in There, Hamlet* into a full length play.

Judith Tullis, "The Poet and The Pauper"

Judith Tullis was born in Chicago and now lives in Indian Head Park, IL with her husband, Lee. She has raised three sons and now enjoys learning about life from her seven grandchildren. Retired from the secretarial business she owned for years, she found a creative outlet in writing poetry, a combination of the economy of words demanded in business writing (her job) and the rhythm of music (her hobby). She is a member of the Brookfield Library Writers Group, Poets & Patrons of Chicago, and is former Vice President and current Treasurer for the Illinois State Poetry Society. Her poems have appeared in several print and online venues.

Cindy Wallach, "Slicker Swap"

Cindy Wallach grew up in New Jersey but doesn't have the accent. She was a sensitive child and has written poetry all her life. She got over that in law school and practicing Workers' Compensation litigation. These days, she's got time for poetry again, and likes to sit around thinking about the things she should have done.

Laurie Whitman, "Not Just Another Coat"

Laurie Whitman wrote the column, "Life in La Grange Park" for the *Suburban Life* from 2000-2009. What she most enjoyed about that assignment was getting out into the community and meeting new people. She takes great pride in La Grange Park, IL, having been a resident for the past thirty-eight years and raising her two children there. Additionally, Laurie wrote for the online newspaper *Patch*. For *Patch*, she continued her column about La Grange Park and also wrote a column entitled "Hunt and Gather" which chronicled how she would purchase a seasonal item at the La Grange Farmers Market, design a dinner around it, and pair the meal with a unique beer. She would share her recipe after stringent testing by her family. Laurie recently appeared in *Reader's Digest* with a 100-word story about her granddaughter. Her blog is www.lagrangeparklive.blogspot.com.

Made in the USA
Lexington, KY
14 April 2016